Imagine This!
An ArtPrize® Anthology

CWG
CASCADE WRITERS' GROUP

Cascade Writers' Group
Chapbook Press
Grand Rapids, Michigan

Vol.1 July, 2013

Cover art: Svelata, by Mia Tavonatti. Second Prize, 2010

Chapbook Press

Chapbook Press
Schuler Books
2660 28th Street SE
Grand Rapids, MI 49512
(616) 942-7330

www.schulerbooks.com

Printed in Grand Rapids, MI

Library of Congress Control Number: 2013946502

ISBN 13: 9781936243617
ISBN 10: 193624361X

Designed by Ronald Kauffman

Ronald Kauffman was born in Kalamazoo and has lived and worked in Grand Rapids for the last 25 years. After graduating from Kendall College of Art and Design in 1991 with a BFA in illustration, he worked for a variety of West Michigan companies. In 2003 he became a freelance graphic designer/ illustrator working throughout Michigan and the United States. He can be contacted through his on-line portfolio at: ronkauffman.carbonmade.com

Acknowledgements

This anthology would not be possible without the generous donations to our Kickstarter campaign by family, friends, and interested parties who believed that this celebration of the written word was an important contribution to ArtPrize®. Special thanks to Justin Vogelar and Kris Vogelar for making the video and managing the Kickstarter Campaign.

Melissa Anderson
Michael Anthony
Anne, Duke & Allie Aversa
Mark & Michele Aversa
Jeffery & Stephanie Barton
Donna Berryman
René Beyette
Nancy Bock
Faith Bogdanik
Chris & Robbyn Boike
Steve Brooks
Mike and Nancy Burdick
Cascade Family Dentistry
Frank Conner & Jan Darling
Pamela-Harmon Daugavietis
William Davis
Marlys Davis
Michael Davis
Cindi and Chuck de Sibour
Don & Betty Dean
Chris and Parry Eckman
Carla Ethen
Bill & Cecile Fehsenfeld
Carol Finke
Forest Hills Presbyterian Preschool
Founders Bank and Trust

Dave and Diane Gaebel
Auston Gross
(In memory of Tugboat)
Amy Henrickson
Albert Herzog
David Hibschman
Ed & Lori Holland
Cynthia Holt
Scott & Pat Howard
Wayne, Michelle & Daniel Hsieh
Deborah Woods Johnson
Jan Kaplan
Mary King
Gloria Klinger
Mary Beth & Clete Laginess
Tammy Lenhardt
Carole LeVasseur
Rose Ley
Loiselle Family
Mara Mackay
Jennifer Marks
Lynette Martin
Ronald & Edna Martin
Jason R. Masters
Marcella J. McCumber
Lisa McNeilley

Acknowledgements cont.

Anne Neme
Patricia J. Nevala
Beverly Oblack
John & Debi Oswalt
Ashok & Terry Prasad
Susan Rankin
Carol Rausch
Laurie Roberts
Bill Rockwell
Arish Rojas
Nick & Sue Sansone
Daniel Schoonmaker
Jane Schwentor
Tracy Sianta
Peter Jonker & Bonnie Slayton
Maurice Slayton
Roger & Laurie A. Soderstrom
Eileen Starr
Robert & Cora Stauffer

Suzanne Stevens
Tom and Leslie Stolz
Wendy Sturm
Renee TerBeek
Jeff & Cody Thornell
Steve Thornell
George & Janice Thornell
Diane Troost
Tracy VanDuinen
Cristina Herron VanWieren
Jacquline Viol
Justin Vogelar
Patrice Vrona
Sara & Bruce Wehr
Marshall & Marilyn Wehr
Leah Weis
Thomas and Rachel Wolf
Mary Ann Zitta

READERS

In addition to the dedication of the members of the Cascade Writers' Group, who spent an enormous amount of time developing the competition and publication of this anthology, we had a number of volunteer readers who faithfully read and scored the wide array of submissions we received—with excitement and commitment.

M.S. Barnes
Caley Bolderson
Kristin Day
Cindi de Sibour
Amy Duffy-Barnes
Irene Franowicz
Kristin E. Graef, M.A.
Kelly Hagmeyer
Karen Legault
David Rein
Norm Taylor
George Thornell
Kari Vredenburg
Linda Weesies
Brenda Wittenbracher
Emma Wolf
Thea Woodnorth

CASCADE WRITERS' GROUP

Lisa McNeilley, Ph.D., *Editor*
Wendy Sturm, *Project Manager*
John Guertin, *Promotions and Art Coordinator*
Rachel Wolf, *Secretary*
Kris Vogelar, *Kickstarter Director*
Michele Smith-Aversa, *Data Manager*
Sara and Bruce Wehr, *Technical Support*
Janice and George Thornell, *Readers*
Roger Meyer, *Reader*
Susan Rankin, *Reader*
Vance McClenton, *Website Developer*

Cascade Writers' Group welcomes you to celebrate with us *Imagine This! An ArtPrize Anthology*. This anthology was created as a way to include the written word in ArtPrize, one of the most successful art festivals in the world. The short stories, essays and poems were selected from over 200 entries, submitted by contributors locally and from across the nation. It also features Cascade Writers' Group members. Part of the proceeds generated by this anthology will go to support ArtPrize.

Find information about the competition at www.anthologycompetition.com.

Contents

| Poetry |

| Honorable Mention |

| Introduction |

What Are We Doing Here?

Lisa McNeilley, Ph.D.

Our family has a tradition of spending New Year's Day at the beach. It all started when Dave and I were on our honeymoon. We hiked through the rainforest of Costa Rica farther than any other tourists and found ourselves alone in a little cove on the ocean. We spent the day on an expanse of creamy sand. Pelicans flew overhead and tiny sand crabs scuttled across the beach. What heaven. Of course, we said, "We should spend every New Year's Day at the beach."

The next year, when we woke up in Kalamazoo, Michigan, we said, "It's New Year's Day. Wouldn't it be great to be on that beach again?" We weren't. We were in the frozen tundra of lake effect snow, practically in the arctic (or so it seemed to us). But for the sake of tradition and a little adventure, we went to South Haven and hiked along the frozen shore, and we have done so every year since. Now we force our children to go, and we try out different beaches along the coast of Lake Michigan.

It's difficult to describe the awe-inspiring majesty of the lake on freezing winter days. Ice floes careen over the water, washed ashore on each successive wave. Snow drifts along the shore like white-white sand that sparkles when the rare ray of sunlight hits. Waves wash over the boardwalk and form jagged rows of icicles along the railing, monster teeth, frozen and treacherous. The side of the lighthouse is covered with a wall of ice, as wave after wave splashes against its towering height and adds a little more water to freeze to the side.

In the face of such magnificence, I feel alternating waves of awe and vulnerability. I have to ask myself, "What am I doing here?" How can I create meaning out of this brief, wonderful, tragic, bountiful existence? Of course, faced with the wonder of creation, people have been trying to answer this question for millennia. And depending on the culture, the answers have been imaginative, varied and often controversial.

Sometimes it's scary to think that we may never really know the truth about our collective purpose as human beings, but in reality this opens up life's possibilities. It means that we have an opportunity to create significance from our existence by doing meaningful things—from loving our families to helping others to pursuing our dreams. We get to make it all up and decide what the patterns of our lives will be. We can splash waves onto our icy lighthouses and see what freezes there and what shape the icicles take.

The ability to make up a life is why writing, why any act of creativity, is vital. Every word, published or unpublished, is a primal scream pulsing through the void and asserting our existence. And we all want our existence to create a ripple or a splash or a tidal wave. We want our words to create possibilities.

So what are we doing here, in this anthology? We are giving writers the prospect of sharing their thoughts, of communicating their creation to others, connecting human to human in a chain of words. Here, writers tell their stories, share their insights and revel in the beauty of words.

The very act of living is a creative gesture, shaping something meaningful out of the amorphous, intangible breath of life. And writing, like all art, takes that creative act and gives it a medium of expression. To comment on, represent, alter, improve, imagine, expand, even ridicule life—that is what writers are doing here. The words sparkle like snowflakes in the sunlight and we scoop them up and pack them together into sentences and stories and poems.

I create; therefore, I am.

This act of writing can be the mere expression of an idea or the act of defiance and transformation that creates change in the world. Writers like Harriet Beecher Stowe (about whom it has been said that Abraham Lincoln asked, "Is this the little woman who created this great war?") create change from the powerful act of telling a story. The words of Upton Sinclair, Betty Friedan and Martin Luther King, Jr. catapulted our world into new views on the poor, women and African Americans. They led the way to political and social changes that have shaped the way we live today. The pen is truly mighty.

The written word has instigated change in the world throughout time because each word, in itself a meaningless series of phonetic representations, is a link in the chain, idea to expression, giver to receiver. We are tied together through our shared understanding of the meanings of words and our ability to comprehend and shape our experience through them.

When a three-year-old tells the bones of the story, "I fell off my tricycle and cut my knee. It hurts," we can see that tiny moment as part of the monumental human struggle. When a friend tells us of the challenges of dealing with day-to-day life or when a parent tells the story of growing up in times of wonder, we see the deep humanity that connects us all.

From earliest history in works spanning from *The Epic of Gilgamesh* to the poetry of Sappho to the philosophy of Plato, every relic of human existence indicates that since humans developed the ability to form words, they have created poetry and have told each other their stories. It is essentially human to connect with others by telling our stories, from answering the question, "How was your day?" to elaborating on "What I Did Last Summer…"

And that is what we are doing here: telling stories, sharing ideas, being human.

Imagine This

KRIS VOGELAR

A poem dedicated to my friends in the Cascade Writers' Group who dare to imagine.

I behold my thoughts
in a bed of rich imagining
while memories knock,
and dreams ache for words
to fill the fresh white canvas of my masterpiece.

Words come–
wrought in a bargain with the soul—
released one-by-one to dance
tethered
mind to heart
pen to page.

Words once rendered
linger in the quiet
hushed and listless,
longing to be lifted
out from the veil of eloquence
to tell my story
tell, so sweetly,
a tale of expectation, hope, and wonder.

| Prize Winners |

Damascus River Reclamation

KATHERINE CHAPPELL
FIRST PLACE

I'll try to explain. I don't know if you'll understand, but I'll try.

When I was a child, the future seemed verdant, green, and full of life. Possibility was everywhere, pouring out of a spigot opened all the way. I lived life, truly lived it, flinging myself into experiences. I could tap unadulterated emotions in simple things—satiation from a ripe plum, the juices dripping down my chin; giddy joy riding double on a bike with my best friend; sheer wonder at the population of a tidal pool, understanding that the world was wider than I'd ever be able to fully comprehend, and that I was part of that vast span. I would spend my days under the sun, running across the grass or lying prone under a tree with the commitment to relaxation only children and animals can seem to accomplish. I dreamed of thousands of jobs I could try, and I knew I'd be good at all of them. At other times, I could imagine becoming the wind or being able to ride on its back until it pulled song from my lungs and I sang a rainbow across the sky.

The older I got, though, the more that verdant life of hope receded from my grasp. The future lost possibility, closed in on me, and became merely the present, gray and hopeless. Simple joys were unreachable. Imagination was mocked or deadened by the reality we are told is more important. All the things I knew I was capable of became all the things I could never do. I learned that I would never be good enough.

They call this growing up.

Growing up felt like dying.

I discovered through words and actions of those who claimed to care that I had nothing special to offer, that only a few can aspire to change the world, even in small ways. I was not one of those few. No genius, no talent, no great love, just an ordinary, space-wasting person, not smart enough to be satisfied with the small, sere existence that is all we are granted. Then debt and failure and illness and all the broken things of life crept in and set up camp, blocking my view of anything that might relieve their pressure. I was sinking into a hole too deep to ever get out. Depression found a toehold in the cracked wasteland that had once been my joy and everything that might have fought back against it had been uprooted.

Finally, I could stand no more. I headed up through the city into the mountains to a bridge overlooking the Damascus River and parked my car carelessly in the public lot, leaving the door ajar and the keys inside, not caring that I tempted fate and car thieves.

I trudged out onto the bridge, right to the middle where countless feet had walked before me, their owners marveling over the expanse, pointing at vistas, taking engagement pictures, imagining where the river would take them. But it was a Tuesday, just before dusk, and no one else was there. My own feet had walked here before, my heart seeking the peace of the water and the trees and the simple perfection of the natural world unchanged for hundreds of years except for this manmade expanse. Today I wasn't sure peace would be so easy to find. I wasn't sure I deserved to.

I leaned heavily against the railing, my burdens pushing against my flesh from between my shoulder blades, pressing me into the metal. I gazed out over the water and found myself wondering if I could simply cast myself over the barrier. I was caught in the thought—flinging my body through the air, flying like a sparrow, drab and gray on the ground, but as majestic in flight as any bird. I would soar through the air and finally my childhood vision would come true.

And if it didn't, if I fell, well, at least then it would all be over. I might not become part of the green and the wind, but I could mingle with the brown, rushing water and that might be just as good.

I pushed backward, so relieved at the feeling of joy the idea brought that I was ready to clamber over the side then and there. One leap and I stopped wasting space.

That's when the skies fell open. I don't know how else to describe it. They just fell open, abrupt and deafening. For a moment, my eyes were dazzled and my brain went stupid with incomprehension. How had I never seen that the sky was not a single thing, but a million doors, like shoji screens or the trap doors under a stage? They all crashed open above me and I saw – I don't know exactly. I still don't know. But I realized the world I'd always hungered for and given up was there after all.

I was stunned. And then hope fell, plunk, at my feet.

That isn't a metaphor. It was solid, tangible, in a heap in front of me on this otherwise normal bridge. It was possibility and pain and power — and I knew it belonged to me and no one else. This was the hope designed solely for me. I could either gather it in my arms and walk into abundant life... or kick it over the side as I fell down to my ending. The choice was mine.

It wasn't really a choice. I mean, what could I have done? I couldn't doom this shining thing; I couldn't even reject it by walking away. Of course I would take it.

With that acquiescence came the revolutionary realization that the burdens I carried were not sewn into my skin. I could release them. The realization made me angry, of all things. I had been lied to—had let myself be lied to, had chosen to believe that these burdens were my lot in life, were all that defined me. I reached up behind me and tore them from my back, hearing them wail in terror. (I swear I'm not making this up). I could feel the cold pain on my back, like something was missing and my skin was still adjusting to being able to breathe and grow, like it had gone numb and asleep and was only just waking up.

I flung them over the bridge into the wind and the lowering dusk where I had so recently wanted to fly myself. And with them went my spirit. I felt it leave. I saw it leave.

For a moment I was terrified.

Only a moment. Then I realized that, though my spirit went out from me, it did not fall. It wheeled on the breezes like a seagull; the splashing waters beneath it would never get it wet. My burdens gurgled under the river's waves, tossing and dragging along the rocky bottom. But my spirit was simply soaring, released from the weight that had been holding it imprisoned for so long. It would come back to me, was tethered to me, oriented like a migrating bird following the magnetic field.

I gathered the effervescent pile of hope and wrapped it around my shoulders like a royal robe. It spilled around me, silky and shining. I sank cross-legged to the boards of the bridge, leaning my cold back against the rail, stretching my feet out before me. The skies were still ajar above me. I closed my eyes, listening with my whole being to the singing that fell faintly through the openings.

Seconds, hours, days later – I don't know exactly how long – it was over. The sky was just the sky, the arias of angels stopped reaching my ears, and my spirit was tucked safely inside me once more. But I knew what had happened.

I know it sounds impossible. I can't explain it, how utterly real it was. Nothing more real has ever happened.

Now I know what's behind the sky, what my soul strains for, what children instinctively understand before maturity begins to strangle them. Now I send out my spirit, letting it wheel freely through the banks of angels in flight. My burdens cannot live for long on my shoulders before they are either smothered by my cloak of hope or I fling them down over the side into the waters of the river.

The green is back and it can never be taken from me again.

Viola Jasper

Susan Szurek
Second Place

John Jasper suffered from headaches. They had always been a source of annoyance but were sometimes made better by the consumption of the illegal moonshine he was able to get periodically. It never occurred to him that the pain was anything more than just bothersome. When the boys ran through the house slamming doors, or Viola was in one of her moods and the headache was present, John would have a difficult time of it. So would Viola and the boys. She began to watch for the signs of an impending headache. When John Jasper suffered, they all did.

Over time, the headaches strengthened and worsened. Whenever Viola suggested that John seek medical advice from Doctor Evans, he just laughed at her.

"That old fake. And what will he tell me? He don't know what the cause is, and then there is another bill to pay. If you ran a decent house and them boys weren't so ornery, then I would be fine." And then John Jasper would continue the rant, sometimes punctuating it with fists, and Viola would grieve silently at her fate, and the boys would remain gone until the quiet in the house told them that it was safe for them to enter.

After a particularly long and futile sales trip, John became so ill with one of his headaches that Viola, daring to defy him, asked Doctor Evans to examine him. The pain was so great that John allowed him to poke around and then asked the old fake for something to cure the pain.

"Where is the pain the greatest? Can you point to it?"

"Is the pain only in your head or are there other areas of discomfort?"

"How much weight have you lost in the past three months?"

John sullenly answered and ungraciously took the white tablets offered him. When he left, Doctor Evans called a colleague of his to discuss what he was fairly sure was a cancer of the brain in the head of John Jasper. There was no cure. The headaches would become worse.

They did. It took a few months. John Jasper lost more weight; he became weaker and angrier, and neither the moonshine nor the white tablets nor both taken together helped much. There were times that John was barely able to sit up or to deliver Viola's necessary marital corrections. Viola tried to keep peace and make meals for her family, but the food she made was often thrown against the wall or her. Soon John was spending most of his time in the bedroom, too weak to leave the bed, alternately moaning and screaming. Viola was helpless and hopeless; her role reduced to bearing the brunt of John's anger and pain. The boys were gone most of the time. The late summer sun with its warmth and brilliance aggravated John, and whatever names he had not called Viola before in the years of their marriage, he managed to spit at her now.

Neighbors stopped by but were sent away. Pastor Jonathan from the Methodist Episcopal Church came to comfort, but stopped making attempts after John told him, during one of his more lucid times, that he was looking forward to Hell and did not need the damn pastor's help in getting there. Viola met her few friends on the front porch and downplayed the ugliness within.

Only Doctor Evans managed to actually get into the house and into the invalid's bedroom where there was not much left to do anyway.

One day, when Doctor Evans came to visit, he brought with him a small bottle. He showed Viola how to deliver the drops to John and how much to give him.

"This is what we doctors call God's Own Medicine," he said to Viola, "and while it will not cure your husband, it will calm him and make him tranquil for a while. I am sorry there is not much more to be done for him. Eventually the pain will take over again and he will need increasing doses of it. I can provide you with this, and it may make your job of caring for him somewhat easier." Doctor Evans hoped to see relief in Viola's eyes. He did not.

"Thank you, Doctor. I appreciate what you have done and promise to pay you for your time and medicine when I can." Viola's sad acceptance was more difficult for Doctor Evans to face than the cancer eating away at John Jasper's brain.

"I will be back in a few days. And Viola…John's pain will get worse. Don't be afraid to use these drops. He won't last more than a week. I am sorry." And he was.

The drops worked for a while, but when John Jasper was awake, the strongest part of him seemed to be his vile vocabulary. He relished using all the words he had learned on his many trips to remind Viola how awful she, the boys, and the marriage were. Viola tolerated the abuse and was thankful John was too weak to attack her physically except for the times she came too near his bed. The pain seemed constant now and to protect her boys, she sent them to stay with a neighboring family. They were happy to go. As she watched them disappear, Doctor Evans drove up and stopped in front of the porch.

"Hello, Viola. I figured you were about out of the drops and I brought more. Let's go in. Let me take a look at John."

Viola stood at the bedroom door as John moaned and Doctor Evans did a cursory examination. He helped John to sip the water and drops. John's yellowish face turned towards the sunlight which did not seem to bother him much anymore. Doctor Evans motioned Viola out, and he shut the bedroom door quietly.

"John will not last much longer, Viola, and he will need more of these drops. Do not hesitate to give them to him as the pain will become almost unbearable. I am sorry to see you go through this alone. Let me get someone to help you."

Viola answered without hesitation, "Thank you, Doctor, but John is my husband and I know what he needs. I appreciate all you have done, but I can and need to do this by myself." There was nothing more to be said, and Doctor Evans picked up his bag and turned to leave.

"I will return tomorrow afternoon. Let me know if I am needed before then. Use what you need of the drops to calm John. He can pass peacefully then." And Doctor Evans left.

Viola stood on the porch and watched as Doctor Evans drove away. She walked back into the bedroom where the late afternoon sun no longer warmed John's face. He lay silent, and a small bubble of spit came out of the corner of his mouth as he breathed heavily. A moan escaped, and he turned his head slowly from side to side. Viola stood and watched. She rubbed her upper arm where the latest greenish bruise was fading, and she tried to remember a happy time with him. No remembrance came. After a while, she went to the side table by the bed and moved it to the opposite wall. She unplugged the lamp, closed the window, and drew the faded flowered curtains across it. She went to the chair where John's clothes had been thrown and took them and his shoes to the closet. She made sure John was covered with the old quilt on the bed. She took the glass from the side table with her as she left the bedroom and closed the door. Viola placed the glass in the kitchen sink, and then moved the creaky rocking chair from the parlor, placing it in front of the bedroom door. She walked back to the kitchen table where the bottle of drops for John's ease had been placed by Doctor Evans, picked it up and, walking out to the front porch, poured the contents into a pile of chickweed that was growing by the steps. She closed the door behind her as she came into the house, placed the empty bottle back on the table, hung up her apron, and sat down in the creaky rocking chair to wait

Other than the sounds from the bedroom behind her, Viola heard nothing that entire night except the creaking of the old rocking chair as she sat in it and slowly moved back and forth. The sky became light with an ashy color, and soon the louder sounds gave way to tired moans and then to heavy breathing, and then to total silence. Viola waited until the gray ash of the sky became dark blue and then bright sunlight, before she stopped rocking. Then she moved the chair back, made some coffee, and prepared for the business of the day.

Syncopated Rhythm

MARY HOLLAND SPRINGER
THIRD PLACE

In silent concentration
He wraps...fluffs...and clips
Working his craft;
An artist at twelve.

Tomorrow he'll stand upon rocks,
Line whipping in syncopated time,
Seeking the perfect rhythm...
The perfect moment...
The perfect prize.

Like a well rehearsed dancer
There is beauty in his movements
This, his religious moment
His quiet spiritual surrender.

An explosion
Of water and light!
A flash of splintered silver
Breaks the surface
Then disappears again.

Line whizzing,
Pole bending,
He jerks and reels
Until at last…
    Smiling
He holds up his prize.

He will forever be
Etched in my memory,
Twelve years old…
Bathed in sunlight…
Silhouetted against
A seductive lazy day
And at peace with his spirit;
Balancing in rhythmic time
Somewhere on the edge
No longer a little boy…
But not yet a man.

| Short Stories |

At Sunset

HANNAH VANDUINEN
FINALIST

Mallory slammed the back door behind her and stomped toward the maple tree at the edge of her parents' property. Even though she was fifteen years old, Mallory still climbed the tree as often as she had when she was five. It was her sanctuary. The first two branches formed a sort of chair if she propped her back against the trunk. She told anyone who asked that it was her reading nook–a less childish reason for climbing–but she rarely took a book with her. After all, it was hard to carry one and clamber into the branches at the same time.

In her makeshift throne, Mallory swept her meticulously-straightened auburn hair away from her face and glared around at the landscape, although most of her attention was focused inward. The sun was setting over her family's farm, casting a warm glow over her pale, freckled skin. The sky was striped in Easter egg pastels, but Mallory barely noticed. She folded her legs into her chest and rested her forehead on her knees. Angry tears started rolling down her cheeks, but she didn't bother to wipe them away.

Mallory had all the usual concerns of a teenage girl–a friend who hadn't been very friendly lately, decisions to make about which hair trend to follow for the upcoming summer months, and a boy at school who'd been smiling at her a lot lately. But after what she'd just seen, she found herself wishing high school took up more of her time.

The back door slammed again. Here it comes, Mallory thought miserably. "Mallory!"

Mallory raised her head and dried her eyes in time to watch her mother appear around the corner, half walking, half jogging toward the tree. The fading sun highlighted her mother's face, so similar to Mallory's own. Everyone in town talked about how much Mallory and her mom looked like carbon copies of each other. If her mom didn't have a few age lines around the eyes, and if Mallory didn't straighten her mass of curls every day, the two could pass as sisters. At the moment, they could almost switch positions–it was the forty-year-old with her face twisted in embarrassment and apology, not the teenager. Nearby, a car started up and backed quickly out of a driveway. Mallory figured she could guess whose it was.

"Mallory!" her mom called again, gasping a little. "Mallory, please, come down here. Let me talk to you."

Mallory sat still and silent. An image threatened to overwhelm her senses: the image of a man, not her father, tucking a strand of hair behind her mother's ear and then kissing her deeply. The two of them, her mother and this man who was not Mallory's father, had tumbled back against the counter, not realizing that Mallory was standing in the doorway less than six feet away. Nothing about it could pass as platonic, although her mother had been saying for weeks that Matthew was just a friend. Mallory shook her head, trying to physically knock the image out of her head.

"Mallory, I didn't know you were home."

"Is that supposed to make it okay?" Mallory burst out. The angry tears threatened to return.

"No, no, of course not!" her mother said quickly. Her eyes were wide, as if she were afraid of her own daughter. "It doesn't make it okay at all. I just wish you hadn't had to see that. Him."

"Yeah, well, that makes two of us," Mallory spat. She shifted a little, letting her legs dangle in midair. A breeze had picked up as the sun crept closer to the horizon, chilling her bare arms. She didn't quite know what to do. As much as she might want to, she couldn't spend the night in her maple tree. Most of her friends were out of town for the weekend for a drama competition, so there was no one in town with whom she could bunk for the night. She had to go back in the house, but the thought of walking through her kitchen, through the house her father had built and Matthew had ruined, had defiled, was so repulsive that it actually made her dizzy. She dropped to the ground and steadied herself against the trunk.

Her mom moved as if to hug her, but Mallory folded her arms across her chest in silent rejection.

"Mallory, sweetie, you have to understand. I didn't mean for this to happen."

"Mean for what to happen, Mom? The affair, or me finding out about it?"

"Well, both. But mostly the affair. I love your father, Sweetie, but he's been gone on business so much lately, and I've been lonely, and Matthew—"

"I don't want to hear you say his name," Mallory growled through clenched teeth. Her mother quailed, on the verge of tears.

"Sorry. I know I can't ever justify it. And I shouldn't try. Please, Mallory, let's just go inside, and we'll find a way to make this right, okay?"

Mallory shivered. The sun was fully set, leaving nothing but a dusky grey light along the tree line. Her mother's plea had struck a chord—not because it made anything better, but because it was so far from the matter-of-fact, no-nonsense solutions her mother usually provided. This new call for an adult collaboration left Mallory feeling ancient and exhausted. This time, her mother couldn't fix anything. There were no Band-Aids or healing words. Silently, Mallory drew away from the tree and started trudging toward the house. Her mom breathed a sigh of relief and followed suit.

Without stopping, Mallory went inside, through the kitchen, down the hallway, and into her bedroom. She closed the door. Part of her was afraid that her mom would try to continue their conversation, but she only heard the door to her parents' bedroom shut. A moment later, her mother's voice came through as a low rumble underneath the door. She was on the phone. Mallory didn't want to speculate about who was on the other end. Each option that popped into her head seemed worse than the last. Her Dad? A painful thought. Matthew? Even worse. She lay on her bed, hugged one of her pillows to her chest, and let her tears flow freely once more. As she cried, she pictured a night many years ago, a summer night when the sunset had been just as spectacular. Her parents had been sitting side by side on the back deck, arms thrown lazily around each other, drinking beer. Mallory, filled with the excitement of being up past her bedtime, had run out among the fireflies to dance beside her maple tree with its moonlit, silver leaves. Thinking back, Mallory clung to that image as tightly as she could, knowing that no matter what happened next, she would never feel as carefree as she had underneath those stars.

Dear Jennifer

Lisa Burgess
Finalist

In a wide valley, at the foot of a snow-covered hillside, about a quarter mile from a busy ski lodge, I sat contemplating the events that led to my predicament. My skis had fallen off and slid away from me at some point after I fell, and I would need to find them soon, before the falling snow covered them and made them impossible to see. And then there was the issue of my leg. It hurt—hurt like hell—and every time I tried to twist it to face the proper direction, the pain screamed through my body and forced me to stop.

I admonished myself for choosing not to slip my phone into my coat pocket as I stepped out of our room that morning. I'd looked at it, fully charged and sitting on the faux mahogany dresser, and I'd thought—nah, I'd opted out of the five-dollar-per-month insurance fee; I'd better just leave it here. Mistake number one.

Or was mistake number one telling the wife that yes, a weekend away together is exactly what we needed to get back on track? "I'm done breastfeeding," she'd said, "and my parents really want to take Sammy for the weekend. Let's just get away, go skiing, forget about our problems." Yes, that must have been mistake number one. I had no intentions of forgetting about our problems. I'd told you, Jennifer, right before I left the office on Friday, that this was going to be my and Leslie's last trip as a married couple, and that I was going to use this trip as an opportunity to tell Leslie that I wanted a divorce.

I'd meant it, too. At least, I did until I got home and saw Leslie, all packed and standing there in our kitchen in her black parka, smiling. I just couldn't stand to see the look that would appear on her face were I to tell her face-to-face that I was leaving—it would be a look combining some sort of shock, and then hurt, and then betrayal, and tears. She might even get quite angry. Even in front of the baby, and I just couldn't stand for that. My alcoholic father had lost his temper on me too many times for me to be that sort of father to my daughter.

I'd decided to just save that conversation for later. Maybe that was mistake number one. Had I been honest with Leslie right then and there, telling her that I wanted a divorce, or at least that I'd been sleeping with Jennifer from Accounting, then I wouldn't have found myself freezing to death on the side of a hill.

Oh, god!

My leg, it hurt like hell. Where was everyone? Someone should have been monitoring the slopes, even those less skied upon—that would have made all the difference. Had those Red Cross skiers paid closer attention to what they were supposed to be doing, then, then I might be roaming this earth today on the two legs God intended for me to have.

But it's the irony of that whole situation that still rankles. One little decision to leave my phone in our room caused so much heartache and suffering. My phone was my sword of Damocles; I'd just never realized my entire life existed inside a glass bubble over which a sword hung by a single hair. Had I known that, I might have never made that one tragic mistake—leaving my "sword" dangling on that faux mahogany dresser, where anyone could call it and anyone could pick it up.

Ahh, Jennifer. Beautiful Jennifer from Accounting. Jennifer who knew better than to call me. But call you did, at the exact moment that Leslie returned to our room to call her parents and check in on the baby. Never mind she hadn't seen me for nearly an hour. She wasn't worried. Had she really loved me, she would have wondered where I was for an hour without her. It was her idea to get away together in the first place, not to get away and ski on our own.

She sure was sorry when she found out that I was lying in a wide valley, at the foot of some wretched ski slope, slowly feeling my fingertips and the toes of my good foot begin to warm as my blood began to freeze. The doctors told me later that they could have easily saved my leg if it wasn't for the frostbite.

To this day I have no idea who found me, or how they got me to the hospital. At some point I passed out, and when I woke up I was in a hospital bed, numb from the waist down, the heart monitor beeping in the background. Leslie sat next to my bed, still wearing her black ski clothes. "David," she started, "how are you feeling?" My head was still floating in a medicated fog. None of this made sense. "David, it's about your leg. The doctors had to take it."

Take it? I remember thinking—swear to god—I remember thinking, take it where? And then, a few beats later it clicked. I looked down and saw the bandaged stump that was now my leg. God, god, oh god! How could he do this to me? I had a wife and a child to take care of. I had a company that couldn't run without me.

But Leslie wasn't finished. She stood up, and I remember the look that came across her face—pity combined with satisfaction. "Okay, well, I thought it would be better for me to tell you about your leg than one of the doctors." She brushed her hands together as if she had just been planting flowers. "I'm going to leave now—I have to finish packing your things."

"Packing?" I asked as my head began to clear.

"Yeah. I spoke with Jennifer, you know, Jennifer from Accounting." She crossed her arms over her ribs and frowned. "You will be her responsibility from now on."

My heart sank, because you and I had only known each other for a few months. I didn't feel ready to move in yet. But I'd need help. I could hire a nurse, but could I afford it? I'd need to pay two mortgages with Leslie gone. Who would take care of me? I couldn't unpack boxes like this. And then my thoughts turned darker: you, Jennifer, were a beautiful young woman at the time; would you still want me like this?

Leslie turned to go. "Wait!" I cried, and in my voice I heard all the desperation of my situation. "I'll change. I'll stop seeing Jennifer. I'll do anything, please." She was my wife, for better or worse. But she didn't turn around. She didn't even stop.

I sank into my pillows, hopeless. An invisible fog of darkness fell over me, sucking my breath out of my lungs. Oh, hell, I thought. This is rock bottom. Fate is a cruel dictator, a sadistic hangman unwilling to let me die. Why, why had I made it all this way, out of my alcoholic father's house, off that ski slope, and through an amputation surgery just to be jilted by my wife of ten years! I heard Leslie's hushed voice in the hall, then footsteps tapping away. She'd made up her mind and she was gone.

But fate is a fickle mistress.

Moments later I heard the click of a woman's pumps grow louder and slower. Then a knock. "David?" The door swung open. It was you. You took one look at me, covered your mouth with your perfect, polished fingers and said, "Oh, my darling!"

I loved you so much at that moment, and I married you the second my divorce was finalized. But I buried my memories of nearly dying in that frozen valley alongside my memories of my failed marriage. I kept them buried there for years, through the birth of our first son, after my promotion, over the course of my father's battle with cancer, until now. Now I've realized that it is the unexamined life that is not worth living, that even in the most wretched circumstances, good can come about.

Life and love are sweet, sweet gifts, Jennifer. Lying in that snow-covered valley, with a broken leg, frostbite eating at my limbs, death breathing its rancid breath down the collar of my shirt, I realized that each moment in this life is a gift. I nearly lost my life and my love that day, and never again will I take a moment for granted.

And that is why, Jennifer, I have decided that it is best for us to go our separate ways. I have found love again with a beautiful woman from HR, and I can no more let this opportunity pass than I can prevent you from finding love again.

Take care, dear Jennifer. The divorce papers are attached.

Mo-Mint-Toes, Please

RACHEL WOLF
FEATURED WRITER

When I was nine years old I used to walk the railroad track that ran alongside our backyard when I got to missin' Momma. She left me with her boyfriend, Arnie, a car mechanic, sayin' he could take better care of me than she could.

"I flitter, Tessa," Momma had explained, "like a butterfly goin' from one flower to another. I can't give you what you want. I'm just not meant to be anybody's momma. You'll be better off with Arnie and his momma, Grandma Effie."

Arnie's okay. He always smells like gasoline, though, and his fingernails have black grease under them. But he's real good to his momma always bringin' her candy from the gas station's vending machine where he works. And he treats me better than my own daddy did wherever he is now. But sweet, grease monkey Arnie isn't my momma and neither is Grandma Effie.

I pleaded with Momma to stay or to take me with her, but she just kept on packin' her clothes. We drove her in Arnie's tow truck to the train station in Detroit. I sat in the middle and put my nose up against the silky flesh of her arm and breathed in her heavenly scent. My chest filled with fluttering butterflies.

Just before Momma left us inside the lobby of the station to board the train on the lower level, I grabbed her at the waist and buried my tearful face in her skirt.

"Please, don't go. I love you." I gulped in air between my loud sobs, but all Momma did was push me back.

"Now stop your cryin' and go over there to Arnie."

I refused to budge so she dragged my dead weight body over to Arnie, then released me at his feet. I looked up in time to see her give Arnie a quick kiss. It looked like two chickens peckin' at each other.

Then she turned and left. We didn't watch her board the train. Instead, I stood up next to Arnie and watched his face looking for some sign that he was going to miss Momma too. He cleared his throat then wiped the tears from his eyes with the heel of his hand. I reached over and put my hand in his. He squeezed it lightly.

Then Arnie looked down at me and in his mild-mannered way said, "Come on, kid. Let's get out of here."

That was six months ago. Momma was right. Arnie and Grandma Effie are good to me. I'd only been living with them one month before Momma left us. But we got used to each other right away.

Grandma Effie doesn't like to cook 'cause it hurts to stand on her heavy

IMAGINE THIS | 31

legs, so Arnie does the cookin'. He makes us toasted bacon sandwiches and tomato soup every night for dinner. Yum.

Our house is known as a hole above the ground. Like the rest of the houses on Factory Row, it is always covered in black soot and smells like dirt. Grandma Effie isn't a very clean housekeeper since her eyesight has been failin' her. She does like to save though. She saves everything, like empty cereal boxes, bacon grease, and empty toilet paper rolls. She makes me use my pencils until they are one inch stubs. I'm nearly writin' with my fingernails before she lets me throw one away.

She even saved Arnie's toes that came off last winter because of frostbite. They're kept in a baby food jar on the fireplace mantel, black and wrinkled and ugly lookin'. Arnie won't ever let me hold the jar, so one time when he had gone to work I snuck a closer look at them. I even opened the jar to take a whiff. Pee-ew! When I asked Arnie why he keeps them he said,

"Child, them's no ordinary toes. Them's Mo-mint-toes."

"Mo-mint-toes? I thought they were just toes."

"Naw. Them's special toes. I lost 'em gettin' frostbite walkin' to work through the biggest snowstorm Trenton, Michigan has ever seen. I worked through two entire shifts before I knew they'd fell off."

I really don't know how Arnie got frostbite just walkin' across the street to the gas station, but Arnie tells the story with such gusto, I always want to believe him.

I don't tell Arnie I plan on takin' those Mo-mint-toes for show 'n tell at school today. In my mind I can see my classmates standing around me waitin' their turn to see those special toes. Maybe I'll make a new friend.

I decide to wait until after Arnie goes to work. This morning Grandma Effie is watching her favorite television show *Queen for a Day*. She's sittin' so close to the screen she could kiss it. I have to sneak behind her walking light as a feather, for her hearin' is as keen as an elephant's. I tiptoe into the living room tryin' to be real quiet but the wood floor creaks and pops. I see Grandma's back straighten up.

"Is that you, Tessa? Are you back in there trying to eat my candy?"

Grandma keeps a box of stale chocolate covered cherries in her underwear drawer as if that's gonna stop me from sneakin' and eatin' one every once in awhile. I stay real quiet and move only enough to breath. Fortunately, Grandma goes back to watchin' the television. I quickly step up on the hearth, grab the jar and with hare-like speed, I race through the kitchen and out the back door.

Once my heart stops thumping, I walk to school with new-found confidence. With these special Mo-mint-toes maybe I'll make some friends. I won't be the lonely girl whose momma left her anymore.

In the classroom, it's finally my turn at Show 'n Tell. I tell Arnie's story with the same gusto that he does.

"That's not true," Bobby Slater, the science boy, challenges me. "You can't work that long before you feel your toes fall off."

"It is true! I have proof."

"What proof?"

"Here!" I whip the toes out of my rusty lunch box.

Everyone crowds around me and gasps at what they see in the glass jar. I revel in the attention I am getting. The bell rings for lunch. One of the popular girls, Lucy, asks me to eat lunch with her!

It's Hot Dog Day. As usual, I can't afford to buy such a special treat. Twyla, the banana curl girl with the always new dresses, buys two hot dogs, two bags of potato chips, and three chocolate milks. Then she buys a roll of Mentos candy for dessert and eats half of it never offering anyone a piece.

Once she's done eatin', everyone will gather around to hear her burp. One time, as a joke, someone pushed me in front of Twyla just as she was about to erupt. I had just enough time to put my hands over my face before . . . I swear my neck snapped back.

Today is an unusually warm spring day, so we are allowed to eat our lunch outside on the playground. I find a swing to sit on next to Lucy and eat my catsup sandwich. Twyla sits on top of the slide to eat her lunch. Some of the other kids try to get Twyla to come down so they go for a slide. She won't budge. With gobs of mustard dripping down her chin, Twyla keeps eating.

Some of the children try to bribe her down with a Twinkie or a cupcake. Nothing is working. As I try to think of an idea that might work, I happen to gaze down at my opened rusty lunch box and see the jar of black Mo-mint-toes. Quickly, I take one out of the jar and run over to the slide.

"Twyla, I've got the new minty, black licorice Mentos. Do you want one?" Twyla's head nods up and down. "You have to slide down to get it."

Twyla comes at me like a monkey going after a bunch of bananas. She grabs the toe right out of my hand and drops it in her mouth before I can pull back. Yikes. I didn't mean for her to eat one of Arnie's Mo-mint-toes. I just wanted to bait her so she'd come down off the slide. Then everyone would like me.

Twyla smiles after eating the first one then puts her hand out and asks for what sounds like, "Mo-mint-toes, please?"

I am tempted to give Twyla the last Mo-mint-toe, but remember Arnie's pride in having them. Ah, what the heck. I'll just tell Arnie that Grandma Effie's poor eyesight caused her to mistake them for a stale chocolate covered cherry.

The kids from my class start laughing as soon as they realize Twyla ate Arnie's Mo-mint-toes. It feels good not to be the one being made fun of. And for the first time since Momma left, I have a friend, Lucy.

Lonesome Whistle

DALE DAILEY
FINALIST

I was only a kid, eight or possibly nine, but I remember that fall afternoon like it was yesterday. I was spending a day with my grandpa, my dad's dad. Grandpa decided he wanted to take me out to the farm, the place where he'd grown up. It seemed important.

I remember we drove out to the farm on a series of roads, each one smaller than the last. When we arrived, Grandpa parked in the drive near the road. For a couple of minutes, we stood by the car and looked around. At first, all I noticed were the overgrown grasses and weeds. Then, beyond that, I saw the tumbled house and barn, both weathered grey.

Finally, Grandpa spoke, "It's been a long time since I've been back. Last time I was here, there were people living in the house."

As we walked up the drive towards the house, two large crows flew up, "Caw, caw, caw." Leaves from the ancient trees that lined the drive had filled the hollowed path. They made a rustling sound as we walked. "Grandpa, why did you live out here? I thought your dad worked on the railroad."

Grandpa put his hand on my shoulder. "Yep, my dad worked on the railroad, on the B & O. He was an engineer, the man in charge of the whole train. His job was to take a train into Chicago, layover for the night, and then bring another train back out the next day. It was a big job."

"But why did you live out here?" I asked.

"My mother died when I was seven. She was a very pretty woman, but I don't really remember much about her. Dad needed a place for me to stay while he was gone, so I moved out here and lived with my Aunt Grace."

"Gee, I wouldn't like that."

"I didn't like it then, but you get used to it. It was a long time ago."

Grandpa motioned towards the barn. "This place has changed so much since I lived here." I noticed the barn had a big hole in its roof. There was a sadness in his voice as he continued. "They always kept the barn up, even before the house. There were lots more buildings back then. Over there was the chicken coop, the granary was beside the barn, and over there was the whiffy. Do you know what a whiffy is?"

"Yes, Grandpa, you told me about them before. You used to knock them over on Halloween."

Grandpa turned and looked across the road and beyond a freshly plowed field. "See those railroad tracks. That's the B & O mainline into Chicago. Dad would always blow his train's whistle, two shorts and a long, when he went by. Whenever I heard it, I'd always run out and wave. I couldn't see him, but I knew he was there. Even after Dad was gone, trains would still blow their whistles when they passed by, out of respect for him, I guess."

We made our way through the grass to the house. Grandpa tested the wooden porch steps before we sat down.

"Aunt Grace was my mother's sister. Her husband, Sherman, was a lot older and didn't amount to much. She kept the animals and a big garden, worked hard to keep things going. Those were tough times. I had chores too, but Aunt Grace always made sure I had some time for play. Did I ever tell you about my pet pig Nelly?"

"Yes, Grandpa." I thought I had heard all his stories, most more than once. "But, didn't you ever see your dad?"

Grandpa shook his head. "Not often. Railroad men are an independent lot. I suppose it was hard for him after my mother died. They say I took after her. I'm not sure he knew what to do with a little boy."

"What was he like?"

"Dad's family came over from Ireland. They were dirt-poor when they arrived. They all worked hard, but could never get ahead. Dad was the last of a whole herd of kids. Because of that, he was a real scrapper—you didn't mess with my dad. But he also liked to pull jokes on people. I remember one time he got me.

"He was working the switch yard outside of town and had arranged to give me a ride up in the cab of his engine. The plan was for Sherman to drive me to a train crossing out in the country and Dad would meet us.

"Sherman and I sat in a car at a crossing on a back road. It was dark, way past my bedtime. I felt, and then heard, the engine coming. It was a brand new Lima Berkshire steam engine. As soon as the train stopped, I ran as fast as I could to the engine. Dad grabbed my arm and pulled me up past the steps into the cab.

"Up in the cab, Dad showed me all the valves and gauges and sat me on a metal stool on the right side. The brakeman was sitting across on the left. He nodded and then continued to look forward onto the tracks. I held the cold levers that controlled the steam. Dad pointed to an overhead cord and told me to pull it. He had a sparkle in his eye and I knew I was in for a surprise, but I pulled it anyway. The steam whistle shrieked and I nearly fell off the seat. We both had a great laugh."

Grandpa chuckled—he seemed to be right back in the cab. "Dad was a railroader through and through. He was a proud member of the International Brotherhood of Locomotive Engineers and always wore his brass union pin. Even on days he didn't have a run, he'd usually go down to the station and play cards with other railroaders. I never understood that." My grandpa took a deep breath, "We better be going."

"Grandpa, tell me about the best time you ever had with your dad."

"Okay, but then we've got to go. One time after the war, Dad took me to the Brookfield Zoo in Chicago. We had free passes on the Capitol Limited, the fastest passenger train on the Chicago route. When we boarded the train, the porter said, 'Morning, Mr. Sam. I see you got your young'un with you today.' Later on, the conductor stopped by Dad and took out his pocket watch. 'Good Morning, Sam. We're running a little late today, but we should be able to make it up.' Dad pulled out his watch, it was a Hamilton model 992, and they compared times. All the train people seemed to know my dad."

"We arrived in Chicago later in the day and Dad took me to a small hotel across from the station. I remember the sign said, 'Nan's Rooms, Just Like Home.' Dad said he always stayed there when he laid over in Chicago. A lady at the front desk with a bright green dress smiled when she saw us. She walked around the counter to greet us and gave Dad a big hug. 'Well, Sam. This must be your boy. He's sure got your blue eyes.' Then, she got down on her knees and held me at an arms-length. 'Your dad is always talking about you. He's mighty proud of you.'

"The Brookfield Zoo was interesting, but I mostly remember that lady saying, 'He's mighty proud of you.' Well, we better be heading home. Grandma will be worrying."

We walked side-by-side back toward the car, more slowly this time, when we heard a rumbling from across the road. A freight train with three diesel engines broke through a clump of trees traveling east.

I yelled, "Grandpa, it's a train!"

"I'll be damned. They still run an afternoon freight into Chicago."

The engine's horn sounded, Brrrrr, Brrrrr, Brrrrrrrrrrrrrrrrrrrrrrrrrrrrrrrrrrrrrrrrr. It repeated it again, Brrrrr, Brrrrr, Brrrrrrrrrrrrrrrrrrrrrrrrrrrrrrrrrrrrrrrrr.

Grandpa ran ahead several steps towards the train. He raised both his arms above his head and waved them back and forth in a wide motion. He continued waving long after the engine had passed out of sight.

I joined him. "Grandpa, was that your daddy?"

My grandpa settled to his knees and held me, tears running down his cheeks.

"Grandpa, you're crying."

"Your grandpa is making a fool of himself."

"No Grandpa, you still miss him. That's okay."

CarrieAnn's Story

JANICE THORNELL
FEATURED WRITER

Two ten year-old girls stood facing each other. Their soccer game had ended in a shouting match.

CarrieAnn Wilson, the taller of the two girls, admonished her friend, "Jackie, you didn't have to kick the ball so hard!" CarrieAnn threw her baseball cap down, allowing her unruly, blonde curls to escape. "You did that on purpose!"

Jackie VanHatten's green eyes glared back at her friend. "I don't care! I'm done! I'm hot and sweaty." Jackie turned and stomped away, her black pony-tail bouncing behind her.

"Jackie, stop! Where are you going?"

"Home! This is a dumb game."

"Come back right now! You have to get my ball!" CarrieAnn ordered.

"Get it yourself!" Jackie yelled as she continued stomping home. She knew that CarrieAnn was afraid of the woods.

"Jackie, if you leave, you're not my best friend anymore."

Jackie stopped at the corner of the garage and gave one final parting shot, "You're mean and I hate you!" Jackie stuck out her tongue and then she was gone.

CarrieAnn watched in disbelief. CarrieAnn sat down and stared into the dark woods. She thought of all the evil things that Alex had told her about the woods, as she hugged her knees and shivered.

From the kitchen window, Anna Wilson, CarrieAnn's grandmother, watched with disbelief at the shouting match. It was the first time she had seen the girls have such a serious argument.

She sighed, "Family problems and this heat have caused this argument." Anna said a prayer for both girls, their families and their friendship.

"CarrieAnn, are you two ready for lunch?" her grandmother asked from the back slider door.

"Yes, I'm ready, but Jackie went home." CarrieAnn brushed the tears from her eyes because she didn't want her grandma to see her crying. Her mom thought she needed a babysitter.

"What's the problem?" asked her grandma, not letting on that she had witnessed the entire fight.

CarrieAnn explained quickly, "For no reason, she kicked my ball into the woods." CarrieAnn was afraid to tell her grandmother the whole truth.

"You should probably go get your ball," Grandma suggested.

CarrieAnn looked anxiously toward the threatening woods. She slowly picked herself up and managed to drag herself past the garden and the storage barn. She was so afraid her teeth chattered and she felt nauseated. When she came to the chain link fence that separated her yard from the sinister woods, CarrieAnn gripped the railing for support.

CarrieAnn moved her hand to the gate latch and shivered. She stood frozen at the gate while she argued with herself. Finally, she convinced herself that there was no other choice; she had to go.

"CarrieAnn, is something wrong?" her grandma asked as she stepped onto the porch and sat on the glider chair.

"I was trying to see the ball from here," CarrieAnn lied, feeling really glad her Grandma was there.

"I'll wait for you," her grandma told her.

CarrieAnn forced a smile. "Thanks." She opened the creaky gate, took a deep breath and reluctantly walked into the woods. Carefully, CarrieAnn crept among the trees, looking for her ball.

"Chit, chit." CarrieAnn froze. A squirrel scampered up a tree and made another unpleasant noise at her. CarrieAnn looked back at the safety of her yard. Tears filled her eyes, her legs turned to rubber and she fell to her knees.

She saw the ball and crawled to it.

The ball was resting by a pile of dirt. CarrieAnn picked it up and clutched it to her chest. She noticed something shiny near the dirt pile. "What's this?" CarrieAnn picked it up while talking to herself. "How did it get here? Oh, it's beautiful. Wait until Jackie sees this; she'll be so jealous." In her excitement, CarrieAnn dropped the soccer ball.

CarrieAnn laughed and told herself, "We're rich. I bet it's worth a million dollars. Now Mom won't have to work while Dad is away. I have to show Grandma." She turned and reached for the ball that had rolled into a hole. She felt something hard and smooth and when she picked it up she saw it was a bone. She dropped it like a hot ember. She glanced into the hole and saw many more bones. Her face lost all color and she screamed, "Help! Help!" as she scrambled to the gate on her knees.

"CarrieAnn!" her grandmother called as she carefully stepped down.

CarrieAnn reached the gate and pulled herself up. "Grandma, help me." Tears rolled down the cheeks of the terrified young girl.

"I'm coming. Are you hurt?" At seventy-five, Anna Wilson did not move as fast as she once had.

CarrieAnn could only point toward the woods as she shuffled toward her grandma. They struggled to the porch and collapsed onto the glider.

After catching her breath, Anna Wilson asked. "Sweetie, what frightened you?"

CarrieAnn tried to talk, "I…I…saw…"

"Take some deep breaths," her grandma told her. She put her arm around the shaking girl.

"I saw…I saw…bones," CarrieAnn whispered, burying her head on her grandma's shoulder.

"Bones?" her grandma asked with a frown. She looked toward the woods and shook her head. "We once buried our dog, Sparky, out there. Maybe that's it."

CarrieAnn was relieved that she had only found dog bones. "My dad told me what a wonderful dog he was, but why is he buried behind our house?"

"Your parents bought this house from me before I moved to Florida."

CarrieAnn remembered what she had found. "How did this get out there?" CarrieAnn opened her hand, revealing the treasure she'd found.

Her grandma gasped, surprised to see her long lost engagement ring. "Where did you find that?"

"In a dirt pile by the bones," CarrieAnn told her.

"That little thief," her grandma chuckled. "I should've known. Sparky was always eating odd things. I took my rings off when I was working around the house. One day my diamond ring was gone."

"Grandma, here." CarrieAnn handed the ring to her grandma.

"Thank-you." Her grandma smiled, taking the ring. "One day it will be yours."

"Me?"

"Yes, because you're my only granddaughter."

"It's so beautiful. I'll keep it forever." CarrieAnn hugged her grandma. "Thanks."

"You know sweetheart, we haven't seen very much of each other the past six years with your father's job and my living in Florida," Anna explained to CarrieAnn. "I would like us to get to know each other better."

"I'd like that." CarrieAnn looked at her grandma and saw the same blue eyes and freckled nose that she had. "I'm glad you were here today. I needed you." She realized how much she had missed her Grandma.

CarrieAnn was quiet and her grandmother asked her what was wrong.

"I miss my Dad; can you tell me stories about him when he was a boy?"

"I'll be glad to tell you those stories and many more."

"What about my ball?"

"Your brother can fetch it when he gets home. I'll get lunch ready while you get cleaned up."

"I need a shower," CarrieAnn said. They both laughed.

"CarrieAnn, why is the door locked? Let me in."

"Sorry Jackie, I forgot I locked it." CarrieAnn opened the door to the woman who was her best friend, Matron of Honor and sister-in-law.

"You should see the yard. It's beautiful. Your mom and dad performed miracles. Alex and I should have gotten married here." Jackie burst in, talking rapidly, as usual. "Why are you crying? You should be happy."

"I looked at my ring and remembered the day I found it."

"Your grandma loved telling that story."

"She did." CarrieAnn walked to the bed and sat down. "I wish she could be here today. I miss her so much. I'm glad I could be close to her the last ten years of her life." Tears rolled down CarrieAnn's face.

"Oh, sweetie." Jackie hugged her best friend. "Your grandma was a beautiful, loving person. We all miss her."

"I know; she was my rock. I wouldn't have made it through the time my dad had to be away or when my mom had cancer." Carrie sobbed.

Jackie grabbed tissues off the nightstand. "You have your memories, plus you get to wear her ring. Your grandma wouldn't want you to be upset on your wedding day."

"You're right. I have many wonderful memories and her ring will be a constant reminder of my grandma's love for me."

Jackie stood up. "No more crying. We don't want red, blotchy faces."

CarrieAnn slowly stood up.

"Hurry, your wedding starts in less than an hour." Jackie rushed off.

CarrieAnn grabbed the picture off the dresser. "Come on, Grandma, I'm getting married today!"

Taffeta and Teeth

DEVIN LAGASSE
FINALIST

Diana stood up, the taffeta and tulle of her large, Princess-style wedding dress shushing together as it settled into the perfect bell shape. She heard the murmur of guests as they passed her dressing room on their way into the chapel, could smell the bland scent of the hot-house roses pinned to her hair and mingled in her bouquet with the more fragrant company of lavender. Her hands shook as she reached for the door handle, a lifetime filled with a man's hard arms and rough cheeks looming on the other side.

Against the brass of the doorknob her engagement ring glittered, a fat diamond surrounded by sapphires, an heirloom from Brian's grandmother. She remembered the heat of Brian's hand as he slid that ring on her finger, the blunt curve of his nails and the dark hair on the back of his wrist as he held her hand tenderly and asked her to marry him. That had been months ago. Now, staring blankly down at her own white knuckles, Diana saw a different hand with cool fingers tipped by tastefully French-manicured nails covering her ring and gripping her fingers with a pleading desperation. That had been last night.

The boom of the organ shivered through the church, vibrating up the door and into Diana's bones. She shook her head, her veil fluttering against her colorless cheeks, and, straightening her shoulders, she opened up the door. With each step she thought of her family and all those little moments that made up a life: her mother making blueberry scones on Saturday mornings; the steadying, guiding hand of her father as he helped her ride her first two-wheeler; the weight of her pink, laughing baby sister in her arms for the first time. Twenty-two years of moments weighed Diana's steps down and grounded her to the stone floor of the church. The frothy lace of her bridesmaids' bustles brought her back to the present. In front of them she could see bright light and a dashing outline of the groom's dark hair, dark suit, the shadowed glimpse of a smile. Diana tried to concentrate on that, on the vague glimmer of perfect white teeth. After all, it was the smile that had convinced her to say yes after that ring had been slipped on her finger. She was a sucker for smiles.

It was a smile that had first attracted Diana to her. It had been Diana's first party and her second big rebellion after choosing a secular college. Amidst the hard press of bodies and sticky feel of beer beneath her shoes all Diana could think of was home. Saturdays at home were quiet. With her little sister gone to Bible study and her parents sitting quietly in the living room, Saturdays had always been days for reflection before Sunday morning service.

There was no introspection here, around Diana music blasted out into the crowd making bodies pulse together, fingers loosened by booze stroked down the arms of strangers or gripped the nearest pair of hips. A fog of something sharp and sweet hovered over the crowd and made Diana sneeze. It was when she had looked up, her nose running and her eyes watering that she had seen that smile.

Soft lips accompanied by dimples, hair the color of old pennies, and eyes that were bright and clear and staring straight into Diana. It had been like sunlight breaking through the clouds. Diana had moved through the haze and shadowed faces toward the light, toward Kara.

The vestibule to the chapel was dark. Diana felt her father's hand through the delicate lace of her wedding dress, fingers roughened by years of work in the military closed firmly and insistently around her upper arm and she took automatic steps forward. He murmured into her ear, words of encouragement that were drowned to incoherence by the shuffle of hundreds of people standing and the grinding of the organ as it shifted into the wedding march. It didn't matter: Diana knew what he was telling her to do. She began the walk into the chapel and the collective gasp and sighs of awe were like a cold, fierce wind. Tears stung her eyes.

This was supposed to be the moment she sought the eyes of her beloved. Brian's eyes were blue, like the sky in June. They were familiar; Diana had laughed into them at five and fancied herself in love with them at fifteen. At twenty she had looked into his eyes and seen only herself staring back across her parent's dinner table and now, at twenty-two, her eyes skittered past Brian's to the second row where incorrigible copper curls played in the light of stained glass windows. As Diana's body moved forward her mind backpedalled frantically to the night before, to freckled, manicured hands gripping her fingers and begging her to say no, to call it off.

It had been a crystalline five minutes in the space of a blurry three hours. Against the backdrop of her parents' shocked faces, Diana had been dragged from her house by her old college friends and draped in Mardi Gras beads, a penis-shaped shot glass had been thrust into her hand already full of vodka and, a small, tacky veil had been jammed into her hair and bobby pinned with clumsy, enthusiastic fingers. Diana had felt queasy even before the shot glass had been pushed to her lips. Counting time with shots, Diana had been in her seventh hour of hell when Kara had grabbed her wrist and dragged her into a dimly lit hallway near the kitchens. Quietly, over the sound of dishes clanking, Kara had clutched Diana's hand, softly cupped her cheek and spoken low and urgent between frantic, desperate kisses. Those sweet words and sweeter kisses had died against Diana's hard mouth, her lips pressed together in a cold, silent line, and gone no further.

While Kara had spoken of love Diana had heard only her father's voice. He had pulled her aside just like this on the night she had brought Kara home for the first and last time. Her mother and sister had seen only a college room-mate and talked to Kara about her major and her dreams for the future. Her father had seen more. He had seen the way Kara's hand lingered on Diana's shoulder and the way Diana watched Kara leave the room with a soft, happy smile on her face. After dinner he had gripped Diana's arm tight, pulled her into the kitchen and told her to end it. He reminded her of God's law and warned her that he wouldn't have her putting the souls of her mother and sister at risk with some liberal arts nonsense.

Blueberry scones and her sister's laughter or the woman she loved.

It had taken months and a parentally approved engagement for Diana to once more feel the light of her father's forgiveness, and these stolen ten minutes with Kara could ruin it all. Pulling her hand from Kara's grip had hurt, the tips of Kara's manicure scraping across Diana's skin and leaving marks. Diana had gone back to the rest of the bachelorette party with her shoulders rigid, the big, silver cross resting on her sternum heavy and familiar while Kara had slipped away.

Another cross, larger than life and wooden dominated the front of the church. Diana's fingers tightened their grip on her father's arm and she glanced up to see the brush cut above his hard jaw and the authoritative set of his shoulders. He smiled down at her, and biting her tongue, she offered him a watery smile back. She turned her eyes to the front and the hard white teeth of her husband.

Requiem for Raphe

WENDY STURM
FEATURED WRITER

You were in the woods on the day you died. I remember the day was dark, drizzling, hazy and cool. You were on Pelee Island in Canada, shooting wildlife and terrain for National Geographic. There were other people shooting on the island that day too. "First Hunting Fatality of the Season." That's what the paper said. "Tragic loss..."

It has been a long, dark year without you. On this sorrowful anniversary, I imagine you are here with me walking through the woods.

This fall day is extraordinary, not at all as it was a year ago today. It is sunny, warm and windy, almost perfect. Perfect in every way but one because you are not here.

Patches of colorful leaves linger on the trees but many have fallen forming a deep blanket over the forest floor. The color vibrates, like surround sound everywhere I look. Shafts of sunlight pierce the lacy canopy of leaves. It's like being part of a stained glass forest in a cathedral in the woods where the sounds echo as I wade through the leaves shin deep in color.

I can feel the crunch of the leaves and the twigs snapping beneath my feet. The air is filled with the moist smell of the earth and I remember the time you told me, "It's the smell of the earth, of things being born, new life. The fecundity of the earth. It's my favorite smell in the world."

I quipped at you, "Your favorite smell in the world is . . .the smell of the earth?"

"It's because it's the smell of life!" You lightly punched me in the arm, "You idiot!"

I smile at the memory and drink in the scent, willing it to become my soul, my birth.

When we walked these trails we would whisper our secrets, and wonder at the beauty of the season. We'd laugh at finding ourselves in the middle of the woods with no tracks to reveal us as if the trees were hiding our footsteps by bowing down to silently sweep our steps away.

Wanting to remember everything, I pause to look and see the undisturbed carpet of leaves surrounding me. I sigh and stare through tears at the hill in front of me and suddenly the thought that there is no sign of our having been there is daunting. I stand for a moment as my thoughts collide one upon the next like a stack of stones. I need to see the path and somehow carve a memory, an epitaph on this forest path. I need to see the evidence of you, the evidence of me.

We've taken this path together so many times. You know this path as well as I do. It leads to all of our favorite places: the library, the grocery store, the hardware, the diner and our nights out for jazz. How I miss you! I chant in low whispers in time with the rustle of leaves as I force myself forward, *I miss you, I miss you, I miss you!* Each step more urgent than the last. I continue my chant as I climb the hill. With each step I sweep the leaves aside to form a wake behind me moving, pushing, chanting. My breath is heavy as I reach the top and I wait a moment before I turn. But I already know what I will see. Slowly, I look behind to see that the leaves have resisted my effort and I decide to retrace the attempt. On the trip down the hill I do a leaf shuffle dance and add arm flapping to exaggerate my effort. I think somehow this will make it all seem less futile. At the bottom of the hill I look up to see. Still no sign.

What do I do now?

Reluctantly, I turn my back to these thoughts and head home. Yet before long, an idea springs to mind. I feel a ping of hope, and a wee temptation forms, to urge me back to the hill.

I'll rake that path! I will rake it, I can rake it! I begin a new chant with every step.

My inner voice argues. *Don't be a lunatic! Just go home. Stop thinking about the path. Embrace the day for what it is. Savor this extraordinary, beautiful, day. Frame it in your mind and heart.*

I walk up the driveway knowing I'm going to get the rake. I'm rationalizing now. *It's not that I'm raking the forest. It's just a short path and besides it would make it safer. Less slippery in the rain and snow.* I can't help asking myself, *Do I have to have a reason for doing this?* Instead, I choose to think of it as a chance to do something for you.

The rake is light and long with wide green plastic tines. I carry it over my shoulder heading back to the path and silently vow to not look until I'm finished. I begin raking the thick layer. The bright leaves on top are airy and light, yielding easily to the rake, but the bottom leaves are heavy and damp. This isn't so easy, but I can't give up even though I feel a little afraid of what I'll see when I look back from the top of the hill.

Within minutes, I feel hot and sweaty from the work and rest to catch my breath. I push on and with each big swish of movement, I heft the leaves to the right and then to the left. My arms and legs ache with every stroke as I work with all my strength, all my heart. Suddenly, feeling self-conscious, I glance around and hope no one is watching and wondering what I'm doing with a rake in the middle of the hill. I imagine what you would say if you were here.

What is it that you're trying to do? Are you trying to keep me here, or are you working through the steps to let me go?

As I press on up the hill, my inner voice now scolds. *Do I really have to have a reason?*

Why can't I just rake the damn path? Just rake. And that simple thought seems to lift my heart. *Just rake.*

I concentrate on the sounds of the raking as the daylight begins to fade. I am part of the sound, part of the path. Reaching the top of the hill, I take a few long minutes to catch my breath and rein in my doubt to face my work. Now I can see a slight but distinct path. In celebration I cannot resist raking all the way down the path too. My heart lifts with each stroke of the rake.

Absolving my grief, releasing my soul as I scratch to reveal patches of earth and further unveil the path.

The evidence of me. The evidence of you.

Hidden Monster

SARAH SEXTON
FINALIST

*There were very few memories that he could bring up from his early childhood,
and most of them were fuzzy. This one, though, was crisp, all sharp edges.*

Dominic was supposed to be sleeping. Mommy and Daddy had tucked
him in beneath the blue quilt. His teddy bear was under his arm and
the rocketship night-light cast soft shadows around the room. The shadows
worried him. They looked like monsters on his wall. Mommy told him that
they were from the trees outside, or his toys, but he didn't believe her. There
was something in his room that didn't belong there. He was sure of it. He
needed to get Mommy or Daddy to come find it. He slid from beneath the
blankets, still clutching his bear and walked softly across the floor. He didn't
want to draw the attention of... whatever it was.

Their voices were soft when he first opened the door. He couldn't
understand the words but he could tell that Mommy and Daddy were angry.
Dominic knew what angry sounded like even when there was no shouting. He
stood in the crack of the open door, hoping that they would stop. It was bad
to interrupt Mommy and Daddy when they were fighting.

Mommy started shouting at Daddy, and she was using her beer-voice.
Dominic didn't like the beer-voice. It was bad. When Mommy talked like
that she got mean. The last time she had hit him so hard that blood came
out of his nose. Then she was really nice and bought him his teddy bear and
promised he wouldn't hear the beer-voice anymore. But now she was using
it again.

Dominic jumped when Mommy screamed. Then he heard a loud thump
on the wall and something like glass broke.

"You're crazy!" Daddy's voice was surprised. "You almost took my head—
Hey, what are you doing?" There was another thump, not on the wall this
time. Something heavy fell on the floor.

He closed the door and raced back to the bed, diving in and pulling the
quilt up over his head. His heart was beating so fast, like the wings on the
little hummingbirds that came to Mommy's birdfeeder. He couldn't catch his
breath and his body shook. The monster must have shrunk itself and snuck
out of the bedroom when he was standing with the door open, then gone into
the other room and got Mommy and Daddy.

Footsteps moved down the hall toward his bedroom. If it came in his
room it would easily find him under the covers. He slithered silently down

to the floor and wedged himself into the tight space beneath the bed. It was good that he wasn't afraid of small places like his cousin Mark.

The door opened a tiny crack. Light from the hallway came through, just a sliver, and with it a shadow. His heart felt like it was coming up into his throat and would cut off all of his air and choke him. Please, please don't look under the bed, he thought. Don't find me!

It opened the door wider and stepped in. All he could see was its feet and the end of Daddy's baseball bat. The monster was wearing Mommy's slippers. There was something yucky on the bat.

Go away! Don't see me! Don't find me!

"Dominic, honey?" It was Mommy's voice, quiet. She was looking for him.

He almost said, "Here, Mommy, here I am!" and flung himself at her slippers, but he didn't. Something was wrong. It was Mommy's voice but it wasn't. There was a sound in her voice, a funny sound that wasn't her beer-voice, and it scared him. The monster was wearing Mommy's voice just like it wore her slippers.

Don't find me! Don't see me! Don't!

"Dominic, I know you're in here." It closed the door behind itself so Dominic couldn't sneak out. "Come out, honey. It's okay. Mommy and Daddy had a little fight but you can come out now."

The slippers moved around the room. He couldn't see much from under the bed, only its feet, but he could hear it moving. It opened the toy chest, the closet, pulled back the curtains and opened the window. Soon, he was certain, it would check under the bed and then he was a goner. The rocketship might not give off a lot of light, but Dominic was fairly sure that monsters could see in the dark.

I'm not here. Not here. Don't see me!

It stood close enough that he could have reached out his short three-year-old's arm and touched the soft slippers if he dared.

"Dom, are you hiding under the bed?" It dropped the bat to get down on its knees. He closed his eyes tightly, willing the Mommy-monster not to see him.

No! No! I'm not here! Don't see me! DON'T SEE ME PLEASE!

He kept his eyes closed and tried to curl into a ball, terrified and trembling. Even if it couldn't see him the monster could probably hear his heart, it was so fast and loud! Any second a hand would grab him and drag him out from under the bed.

It never did. Footsteps moved away from the bed, then down the hallway. The front door opened and closed. A draft of cool air from the open window slid across the floor and tickled his toes. He was afraid to open his eyes. Dominic stayed curled under the bed thinking, "Don't see me!" until he fell asleep.

He woke up to the sound of his name being called. It wasn't nighttime anymore. Please don't see me!

He peeked out from under the edge of the bed. The feet he saw were not wearing Mommy's slippers. They were Daddy's feet. Slowly he crept out of his hiding spot. Daddy glanced right past him, calling his name. Why didn't Daddy see him?

"Daddy!" he yelled. He ran to Daddy and wrapped himself around Daddy's legs. Strong arms scooped him up and held him close, and his fluttering heart finally slowed.

That had been the most terrifying night of his life. Even now, twenty-five years later, the memory still made his heart race. He had learned something important about himself, though. Dominic could make himself invisible merely by wishing it so.

Beast of the Woods

SARA WEHR
FEATURED WRITER

The seasons were turning and all was as it should be, or so it seemed, as I tipsily tripped my way along the road through the woods that led to my home. Dark and dense, these woods could stand a person's hair on end even in the daylight. But the moon was strong this night, and my long association with this copse had given me a brazen confidence in passing here. I danced along, bellowing a song.

Now on occasion, as I traversed these woods, I had heard rustlings; of course there were rustlings – it was a wild place and many animals called it home. So when it happened that a twig snapped off in the woods to my right, I gave it only a passing thought. It was probably a deer disturbed by my intrusion at this late hour.

The community harvest celebration had been worth the inconvenience of this late return. I had shared numerous flirtations on the dance floor with many of the lovely, and a few not so lovely, but available girls. With no one around to see, I chuckled and whirled in the road to a tune still playing in my head and the memory of one particularly sweet body pressed closely with mine. Perhaps I would be paying her a visit in upcoming weeks to further our association.

The friendly light of the moon was only a faint glow behind me, and had yet to appear to the fore; it would be some long minutes before it would reappear to guide my footsteps out of the woods. Again I heard a snap and a rustling to my right, this time a bit closer. I stopped to scan the shadows. The woods around me were silent and I could make out no movement, nor could I identify any threat, so I dismissed it as I had before. It was likely a forest creature heading for the creek that ran through the fields and past my home. It was not unusual that wildlife would be heading to water in the open this time of night, or so I reasoned with my budding fears. With no further disturbance, it was not long before I resumed my foolishness, savoring remembered amusements, my feet crunching and scraping loudly over the dirt and gravel of my way. Hard cider had been plentiful, of which, I admit, I had partaken generous share.

The darkness of the woods solidified here where the trees grew dense, branches interlacing tightly as though attempting to entrap unwary travelers, thus I knew I had made it halfway through. The thick murk caused me to adopt a more sober attitude and focus on each step. Once again scuffling sounded from the brush, this time much louder and nearer than it had been;

whatever was moving through these woods with me appeared to be on a trajectory that would soon intersect mine. I paused only briefly to listen and heard no more; even so, I hastened my pace. Gone was the merrymaking in my thoughts, replaced with a growing desire to have the moon lighting my way again.

A few more minutes passed and I heard the disturbance again, this time far closer. Too close! Heavy footfalls gave some indication as to its proximity and – was that a grunt? The hairs on my neck and arms began to rise and my feet needed no more provocation to take flight. If I could just make it out of the woods, I'd be able to identify my pursuer, then I would surely laugh at my own foolishness when it proved to be some animal innocently on the same trek.

On I ran through the darkness, and now I was certain the thing followed me, the commotion it made as it trampled through the brush in pursuit convinced my feet to further haste, and I was able to put some distance between us.

My eyes searched ahead of me, desperate for the moonlight that would mean the start of my cleared lands. Surely the beast would not follow me into the open! My breath came in gasps as exertion, distance and fear all took their toll. I did not allow them to slow me. No! I let the sounds behind me and my fears drive me to new velocity as I rounded a bend, and finally saw the distant light of the moon that marked the transition from woods to field.

From behind me rose an unearthly cry; the sound of something on the prowl that recognized its prey was escaping. Footfalls on packed earth informed me that the beast was now using the same road as I, and closing the distance.

In terror, I put on speed I did not know I possessed and pelted through the darkness for the ever closer light. Behind, I could hear the growling breaths of the beast that pursued me, much too near for my comfort. My tiring legs could give no more! Very soon I would gain the moonlit open and that hope spurred me on.

Nearer and nearer the lit egress came but I felt the unknown monstrosity behind, close enough to strike at me and miss. No matter my fear and the danger I knew I was in, I simply could go no faster! Another moment and I felt the beast's claws rake through my shirt. A searing pain cut my back on a diagonal from shoulder to hip. I would have cried out but had not the wind to spare. Teeth snapped close to my shoulder and I could feel its hot breath! It was only with the greatest of contortions that I was able to elude its grasp.

Bursting from the woods into the light, I did not slacken my pace, nor stop to identify my attacker. I veered sharply, leaving the road behind, cutting short the distance between myself and the imagined safety of home. Sparkling in the moonlight, the creek ran silver between two low hills – I'd have to ford it, having shirked the longer path and the bridge. That was my next goal.

Behind me, I heard the beast stumble, earning me some room, and still I ran as fast as my failing limbs could carry me. The weighty cadence of its stride betrayed to me that this was no animal I had ever encountered before this night, and a morbid curiosity to set eyes on my attacker gnawed at me. It was the stronger emotion, fear, which kept my sight ahead.

I heard my pursuer closing again as I dove headlong down the small rise, throwing myself into the water. I thrashed my way toward the opposite bank. The water was frigid but welcome as my body was heated from my lengthy flight. Behind me the beast shrieked its frustration in a voice not of this world.

Crawling out on the far bank exhausted, I finally allowed myself to look on my pursuer. My vantage was such that all I could see was a dark silhouette racing for the only copse of brush near at hand. Was it human or animal? I could not say one or the other for certain. I lay wet, cold and gasping for breath in the moonlight, allowing myself to feel some small relief as I watched it retreat. It seems the water had proven some kind of barrier to the beast, one I didn't choose to question. Once under cover, it turned its red, glowering eyes on me, and the seething malice I saw there drove me to my feet again.

I do not know how I arrived home that night, but I awoke in my bed, still in my tattered clothes. I would have passed the whole thing off as a cider-soaked dream until I sat up, and the bed linens painfully peeled away from my torn back. What happened that night, I cannot say for certain, but of the reality of the beast's existence, of that I'm sure. What came so close to preying on me remains a frightening mystery.

Never again would I keep such late hours nor imbibe as much as I had on that occasion. I adopted a habit of being safely indoors with candles lit and my fire well stoked before sunset. On occasion, when the moon shines strongly, I'm certain I hear the beast's ungodly cries in the distance, a sobering encouragement to keep my cautions.

| Artist Biographies |

Cover Art, Svelata by Mia Tavonatti, *ArtPrize® Second Prize, 2010*

Mia earned her BFA and MFA from California State University Long Beach, where she majored in illustration. She has also studied in Paris at the Sorbonne, Parsons School of Design, in the studio of renowned French impressionist Monsieur Relange, and in Italy and Greece. Mia has also had work chosen for exhibition at the American Museum of Illustration in New York and by the Los Angeles Society of Illustrators for their annual juried exhibitions. In 2007, Mia moved to Italy to unveil her humanitarian project *Svelata*, a monumental series of oil paintings on canvas at the ancient Museo Arsenale in Amalfi. In June of 2008 Mia was one of twenty artists chosen worldwide for an exhibition at the Cesi Palace in Acquasparta, Italy, where she was awarded "Best of Show." Mia has since returned to California and has formed the *Svelata Foundation for the Arts*.

Rebirth of Spring, Frits Hoendervanger, *ArtPrize® Third Prize, 2012*

Born in the Netherlands in 1947, Frits became interested in art at an early age. Since 1964 he has lived in Michigan. A self-taught artist without formal training, he has nonetheless received numerous awards for his painting, and is represented in both public and private collections including the Michigan Governor's mansion and the collection of former President Gerald R. Ford. In 1989, he received a major commission from Booth Newspapers to create a mural depicting the history of The Grand Rapids Press. The artist is best known for his paintings of vanishing Michigan landscapes.

Metaphorest, Tracy Van Duinen, Todd Osborne, Phil Schuster, *ArtPrize® Second Prize, 2011*

Tracy Van Duinen
Tracy Van Duinen was co-lead for the 2nd place 2009 ArtPrize® entry *Imagine That*. He has recently completed *Happiness Is* for the Helen DeVos Children's Hospital Lobby. Van Duinen, a Kendall College of Art & Design graduate, works in the Chicago Public Schools using public art to help urban teenagers connect with their community.

Todd Osborne
Todd Osborne is co-lead for Imagine That and Happiness, which is at the Helen DeVos Children's Hospital. He has been teaching art on the South side

of Chicago for the past six years. Osborne and Van Duinen have been working with inner-city youth to create large-scale multimedia murals on blighted underpasses and playgrounds all over Chicago.

Phil Schuster

Phil Schuster is a sculptor with over 25 years experience in creating bas-relief sculptures and public art environments. Schuster has made innovative works involving communities of large scale, site-specific artworks. Schuster has made dozens of unique art installations, creating whimsical concrete gardens in urban spaces.

Nessie on the Grand by Richard App/Tom Birks/Joaquim Jensen/ Michael Knoll/David Valdiserri, *ArtPrize® Sixth Prize, 2009*

Richard App

Richard App, born in Reykvik, Iceland, has owned and operated the Richard App gallery for 18 years. Clients range from residential to large commercial entities including all three Grand Rapids hospitals and several downtown law offices. He earned his BFA in Fine Arts at Kendall College of Art & Design in 1991.

Thomas Birks

Thomas Birks is an animation designer and editor for HiDef content with a background in illustration and film production. He also designs and builds furniture and does prototype work. He earned a BFA in illustration from Kendall College of Art & Design in 1986.

Joaquim Jensen

Joaquim Jensen was born in Oslo, Norway, and is owner of Dygon Design & Product Development, specializing in office furniture. Joachim earned his BFA in Industrial Design from Kendall College of Art & Design in 2000. He lives in Grand Rapids.

Michael Knoll

Michael Knoll is a fine artist who strives to reproduce textures and colors found upon man made or naturally occurring objects. The impact of light upon surfaces inspires his techniques and determines the materials he uses to achieve his intended result or illusion. The materials can range from paint and charcoal to wood and steel along with a multitude of other elements depending on the project. He has had the opportunity to work in gallery settings and public displays in both 2D and 3D. Michael earned his BFA from Grand Valley State University with an emphasis in oil painting.

David Valdiserri

David Valdiserri was born in Saginaw, Michigan. He is an award-winning designer and specialist in seating design and development. David's design career began in 1987 while at Kendall College of Art and Design. His work has been featured in *Metropolis, Contract Design* and *Interior Design Magazine.* His awards include a Best of NeoCon Silver for the Bernhardt "Pilot" Chair in 2006, and Silver for the Flip Chair at the China International Furniture Fair (CIFF) in 2009. He earned his BFA in Industrial Design from Kendall College of Art & Design in 1990.

Parsifal or Steam Pig by Tom Birks/Joaquim Jensen/Michael Knoll, *ArtPrize® Ninth Prize*, 2010 (See above).

The Rusty Project by Ritch Branstrom, *ArtPrize® Fifth Prize*, 2011

Branstrom is recognized as an award-winning artist with numerous publications and national "Best of Show" awards, most notably at the Kentucky Festival of the Arts in Northport, Alabama; Cain Park Arts Festival in Cleveland, Ohio; and the Kohler Midsummer Festival of the Arts in Sheboygan, Wisconsin. His work as an artist has also led to a seat on the Governor's Board of the Michigan Council for Arts and Cultural Affairs. Born in 1967 in Dearborn, Michigan, Branstrom was heavily influenced by the people and places of his surroundings. The two opposing landscapes of the upper and lower peninsulas of Michigan continue to inspire much of Branstrom's work: lower Michigan, with its automotive industry, and upper Michigan, with its rustic and natural beauty. He graduated with honors from Northern Michigan University with a BFA in product design and a MA in 1993.

Grand Rapids Urbanica by Frederico Farias, *ArtPrize® Entry, 2012*

Frederico Farias is an artist living and working in Grand Rapids, Michigan. Primarily an acrylic painter, he also works extensively with mixed media, other types of paint and techniques, (like watercolor, airbrush, pencil, markers). Raised in Argentina, he studied Graphic Design in Venezuela, where he got his BFA in Graphic Design and Illustration. Shortly after graduating he moved to the U.S. where he discovered his passion for abstract painting. Since then he spends his time in his Grand Rapids studio creating and painting. His work is included in numerous collections in the US, Canada, Europe and South America.

Wasteland IC IV by Eric Celarier, *ArtPrize® Entry, 2012*

Eric Celarier has an MFA in Drawing, University of Cincinnati (1997), BA in Art, University of Maryland (1993), and a BA in Art Education, University of Maryland (1991). Celarier has had his work displayed in numerous gallery shows, including Capital Arts Network, a group show juried by Judith HeartSong 2013; Sculpture Now 2013, Honfluer Gallery: a group show collaboration with Washington Sculptors Group, curated by Florcy Morisset; Vivant Art Collection, Philadelphia 2013; and Black Rock Center for the Arts, solo show in the Terrace Gallery 2011. His awards include Best in Show at Those Who Can Teach: MAEA's Annual Art Show 2012; Best Assemblage at Wide Open 3, Brooklyn Waterfront Artist Coalition 2012; and Award of Excellence (Best in Show) at Borders: Visible & Invisible, Nassau Community College 2011.

Tuskegee Airmen by Andrew Woodstock, *ArtPrize® Entry, 2012*

Andrew Woodstock received his BFA from the Kendall School of Design in Grand Rapids, Michigan. In 2012, "Tuskegee Airmen" placed in the Top 50 at ArtPrize®. Andrew's honors and awards include being a featured artist at the Society of Illustrators in New York City and winning two ADDY Awards for Excellence in Illustration. His work has also been featured on the cover of *Moody Monthly* at Moody Bible Institute in Chicago. He lives with his wife Sherry in Plainwell, MI and owns Woodstockarts Design & Illustration.

Cavalry, American Officers, 1921 by Chris LaPorte, *ArtPrize® First Prize, 2010*

For Chris LaPorte, drawing has been a life-long commitment. He has received art degrees from Aquinas College, La Coste Ecole de Beaux Arts, and the New York Academy of Art. LaPorte has taught drawing at GVSU, GRCC, Kendall College of Art and Design, and Aquinas College as well as educational institutions in New York and Michigan. He owns a caricature and portrait business, which has supported his education, travel, and fine arts studio. Through his work, LaPorte has drawn close to 85,000 people over the last 18 years of drawing.

Untitled No. 1, or "Bed" by Jennifer Cronin, *ArtPrize® Entry, 2011*

Jennifer Cronin was born and raised in Oak Lawn, Illinois. She attended the University of Illinois at Urbana-Champaign, where she earned a BFA in painting and art education, while also pursuing her interest in psychology. During this time, she developed an interest in psychological dramas that present themselves within domestic spaces. This interest eventually became the subject of her paintings. As the capstone of her education, she studied painting at Camberwell College of Art in London, completing her education in March of 2009. Since graduating, Cronin has exhibited in many venues throughout the Chicago area, as well as nationally and internationally. She continues to paint in her studio at the Fine Arts Building in Chicago.

| ArtPrize® Artwork |

Rebirth of Spring by Frits Hoendervanger, Third Prize, 2012

Metaphorest by Tracy Van Duinen, Todd Osborne, Phil Schuster, Second Prize, 2011
(Photo by Dennis Grantz)

Nessie on the Grand by, Richard App, Tom Birks, Joaquim Jensen, Michael Knoll, David Valdiserri, Sixth Prize, 2009 (Photo by TJ Hamilton, published Thurs. Mar 1 2012. Copyright 2012 MLIVE and The Grand Rapids Press. All rights reserved. Used with permission of MLIVE and The Grand Rapids Press).

The Rusty Project (with detail photo) by Ritch Bronstrom, Fifth Prize, 2011

Grand Rapids Urbanica by Frederico Farias, Entry, 2012

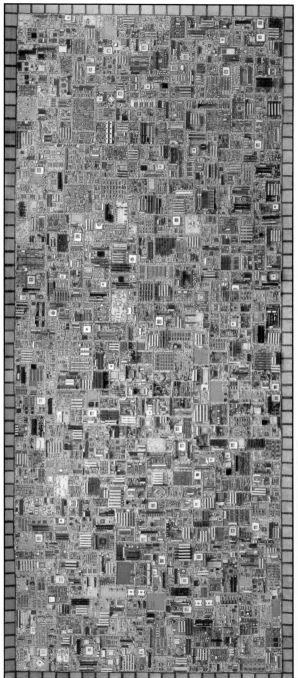

Wasteland IC IV (with detail photos) by Eric Celarier, Entry, 2012 (Artwork photo by Jim Vos)

Calvary, American Officers, 1921 (Detail) by Chris LaPorte, First Prize, 2010 (Photo by Brian Kelly)

Parsifal or Steam Pig by Tom Birks, Joaquim Jensen, Michael Knoll, Ninth Prize, 2010

Untitled No.1, or "Bed" by Jennifer Cronin, Entry, 2011

| Essays |

One Secret

Catherine Keefe
FINALIST

This hour I tell things in confidence, I might not tell everybody, but I will tell you.
Walt Whitman, "Song of Myself"

I saw Angel today, Walt Whitman's birthday.

He sat slumped in the driver's seat of his sagging brown Dodge truck in the General Store parking lot at ten in the morning guzzling beer from a 24 oz. can. His head waggled and seemed disjointed from his neck. His red eyes blazed. When I jumped out of my car and tried, after all these years, to finally thank him he waved me away with a wobbly hand.

"No, no, no."

What is a man anyhow? What am I? What are you?

I'd hired Angel one winter to mow my grass and pull weeds, to prune my roses and feed the orange trees. He did those things sporadically and not particularly well. His strength was drinking beer and surprising me with gifts. His specialty was to plant what appeared to be utterly dead fruit trees in my yard.

"The other house, don't want," he told me the first day I came home to find a bony trunk with naked branches staked on the fringe of my grass.

"What is it?" I asked.

Angel spread his muddy palms to the sky and shrugged.

"Fruit."

"What kind of fruit?"

He spread his muddy palms to the sky and shrugged.

Slowly a patchwork orchard emerged. Angel murmured to the branches as he hand watered the circles of dirt around each tree. When he caught me watching, he smiled broadly.

In all people I see myself, none more and not one a barley-corn less,
And the good or bad I say of myself I say of them.

"Is it alive?"

Angel nodded, yes, always yes.

"What kind of tree?" He spread his muddy palms to the sky.

Each tree ignored my need for it to prove its place by greening, then blooming on any proper schedule. I researched the rhythm of bare root fruit, but spring didn't bring an end to the mystery. The trees remained unfazed as earth turned toward blooming season. I stopped inspecting the branches after a while and began instead to consider how hard it might be to pull up dead trees.

Then one damp night I was restless and wandering, wanting stars.

Solitary at midnight in my backyard...

Angel's first tree shimmered in the moonlight. I walked up to it and swear I heard trumpets. What I'd missed all those days, looking from afar at the branches, barren of leaves, was the riot of ruffled pink popcorn pearls pinned on slick branches. Tight blossoms were poised this night to begin a wild unfurling.

Peaches? Apricots? Nectarines?

What could I imagine eating sun-warm some months from now? What might I capture in jam jars to tie with red gingham?

Earth! you seem to look for something at my hands,

Say, old top-knot, what do you want?

The next time I saw Angel and showed off our blossoms he smiled, more bemused at my excitement than joyful for the harvest. I'm sure he never doubted fruit would come. A peach tree. An apple. An orange. Another apple. A plum. An apricot.

For seven years Angel tended our slowly growing orchard. His faith in the indiscernible life hiding within brown leafless branches scavenged from rejection was impeccable. Then one day Angel stopped coming. Yet still every now and then a new barren tree would appear and I'd look over my shoulder, half expecting to see him squatting at the base of the apple tree, his favorite spot, humming absently.

If you want me again look for me under your boot-soles.

I began to wonder if I'd imagined the man. When he called himself Angel was that a name or his being? I took over the care and feeding of the trees and silently thanked him with each basket of ripe fruit I brought into my kitchen. I shared the bounty with neighbors and told them about how Angel showed me you could save a thing by moving it to the right home and tending it with water and words. Was I creating a myth?

You will hardly know who I am or what I mean...

Today as I walk back to my car, rebuffed, I turn my palms to the sky and shrug. Driving away, I wonder. If I could plant Angel in my backyard would he bloom again?

Author's Note:
The words in italics come from Walt Whitman's "Song of Myself (1881)

Outsmarted by Pinheads

MICHELE SMITH-AVERSA
FEATURED WRITER

I've recently heard of a new trend. Something about eating healthier. I admit I'm suspicious of foods that are grown in the ground (barbaric), sit in the grocery store without the safety of a Styrofoam and plastic barrier (unsanitary), and are readily enjoyed by large populations of rabbits and deer (I am not a forest animal). However, despite my fears of leaving behind my steady diet of saturated fats, hydrogenated oils and processed sugars, my doctor recommended (nay, threatened) that I give the new trend a try.

So, I started with breakfast. I tried bran cereal, Greek yogurt and fruit-and-fiber-frosted-shredded-nut-oat-chewy bars that tasted like high fiber cardboard. Finally, I tried oatmeal. Beige, lumpy, disc-shaped globs of goodness – yuck. I tried it with variations of butter, milk, molasses and raisins. Not much better. I even tried soaking the raisins in rum. That wasn't the answer either, although rum is now a part of my morning ritual.

One day, a friend suggested I try steel-cut oatmeal, also known as pinhead oatmeal, thinking that the chewier texture would appeal to me more than a bowl of goo. She explained that it cost three times as much for ¼ of the volume, so right away I knew it was superior.

Taking out a second mortgage on my house, I went to the grocery store. Using my opera glasses, I found a miniscule container of this steel-cut gift from the Nature Gods behind its much larger but flattened, instant-cook brothers.

I rushed home, anxious to try it. I read the container: ¼ cup oatmeal to 1 ½ cups water. That couldn't be right. The ratio for "normal" oatmeal is 1 to 1. So I read the container again. It still said ¼ cup oatmeal to 1 ½ cups water. Wow, that's quite a ratio of dry to wet ingredients. Those little pinhead-pellets were going to have to puff up like a water-retaining hippo suffering from PMS on a humid day in the rainforest. This stuff sounded more like odds on a longshot at Churchill Downs – "6 to 1, put your money down to win!" If only I could bet on my oatmeal. The ride to the finish line (a perfect bowl of steel-cut oats) would prove to be just as bumpy.

Day 1 – I entered the kitchen with inspiration in my heart and a growling in my stomach. I consulted the back of the container again. Stovetop or microwave? Wanting to use the method that had been perfected over hundreds of years, I chose the old-fashioned stovetop method. I placed the saucepan on the burner, mixed the two ingredients together and started stirring. The container directed to bring the mixture to a boil, then stir constantly until your arm fell off or a half hour, whichever came first.

I felt my enthusiasm waning. Half an hour can seem like an eternity if you are stirring something non-stop or you are a hostage in a bank hold-up. However, since the package pledged a breakfast utopia of thick and hearty oatmeal so phenomenal that I would sell my firstborn child for a bowl, I stirred on. I am not one to turn my back on a promise of food that incredible.

At the end of the 30 minutes, arm still intact but now twice the size, I stared into the pan. Percolating away was a light brown mixture with tiny, hot, steel-cut pebbles swimming around, mocking me. I decided to alter the instructions and let the mixture bubble solo for the next 20 minutes while I sat at the kitchen table pondering Communism and black holes, the latter being where the last half hour of my life had disappeared. After 20 minutes, I thumped a bowl down onto my counter, grabbed the pan and poured the Pinhead Soup into the empty receptacle. I threw in a little bit of brown sugar and ate the concoction with a soup spoon. After spending almost an hour in the kitchen, I expected the oatmeal to be fluffy, creamy, chewy and gooey with a nutty taste that danced around my tongue and made my tastebuds sing to the heavens – instead of this bowl of faulty fodder in front of me.

Just then, my husband came into the room and asked how my breakfast was. I poured the liquid off my spoon. He just shook his head. He knew.

Day 2 – I entered the kitchen with trepidation in my heart and a growling in my stomach. I read the back of the container again. Stovetop or microwave? I wasn't messing around today, so I chose the nuclear approach – the radioactive invention of the microwave. Maybe a change in cooking method would result in a speedier finished product that was a cut above – get it?

The directions said to use ½ cup of oats (vs ¼ cup for the stovetop), 2 cups of water and put it in an 8-cup container. I laughed. Why on earth would I need a vessel that large? However, my personal rule when cooking something new is to follow the directions to a T. Or in this case, to a dead end.

I poured the double serving size of oats and water into the huge glass bowl. Covering it with plastic wrap, I set the timer for five minutes. When it was done, I pulled out the bowl, peeled back the plastic wrap, ducking the steam so quickly even Mohammad Ali would have been impressed. The concoction looked the same as it did five minutes before, with water on top and oats on the bottom. Regardless, I stirred it, which was as effective as stirring rocks at the bottom of a fish tank, put the plastic back on it and hit full power for another five minutes. The directions stated that the meal should be ready at this point, except for the losers out there with underpowered microwaves. The politically correct way to say this is "microwaves vary in size and power. Cooking times may need to be adjusted." But we all know what they mean. Just hand us our scarlet letter "L" and let us get back to our inferior, underpowered cooking boxes.

After the five minutes were up, I looked at the microwave. Scrolling across the display was, "Food is ready…Food is ready." I rolled my eyes at its chirpy optimism. I opened the door and pulled out the bowl. The plastic wrap had melted like Swiss cheese under a broiler and yet the mixture (I use that word facetiously) was still top-half water, bottom-half oatmeal. I stirred it - at this point I stopped asking myself why - put the bowl back in the microwave uncovered and set the timer for five more minutes. After only one minute, the water bubbled up to the very top of the 2-quart bowl. I yelped in surprise and yanked the door open. The bubbles quickly receded, as if they'd been doing something wrong and I'd caught them in the act.

Frustrated, I decided to finish up back on the stovetop. I placed a small saucepan onto the range, poured the mixture into it and turned on the burner. A cooking show I'd seen once suggested to cover and simmer it on low heat in lieu of stirring. There was nothing to lose at this point. I dropped on the lid, set the timer and went into my office to work.

When the timer dinged, my stomach growled with excitement; however, I had mixed feelings. The pinheads had already been too much trouble, but I was looking forward to a hearty breakfast. Walking back into the kitchen, I stopped and gaped at the sight before me.

There, on the smooth flat cooktop, was a gooey substance under the pan, cooking directly on the burner. I lifted the lid and there was absolutely no liquid in the pan, only a large beige ball of oatmeal. The water gods must have grown weary of my whining and boiled all the water out! I cursed Poseidon and then spooned the beige grain balls into a bowl. This uncovered a burnt layer stuck to the bottom of the pan. Good grief! I got tired thinking about the hours of soaking and scrubbing my husband had in front of him (jealous, girls?). Okay, that isn't fair. Poseidon was angry with me, not my husband. I set the pan on the counter and grabbed a butter knife, planning to chip away at the burned bottom. Tucking the knife under the edge, I was shocked when it lifted right up! It peeled out in one big circular piece, leaving the pan perfectly clean. It looked like a silicone disk.

Setting the oatmeal Frisbee in the sink, I stared at my food. Now it was too dry. I just couldn't win. A little milk and a spoonful of brown sugar later, I had myself a petite meal. My husband came into the room at this point and asked how my breakfast was. I went over to the sink and held up the beige disk. He just shook his head. He knew.

Day 3 – I entered the kitchen with defeat in my heart and hunger in my stomach. I prepared my breakfast and sat down at the table. My husband walked into the room and asked how my breakfast was. I showed him my plate of Oreos and small glass of rum. He just shook his head. He knew.

The Wedding Shower

LEZLIE WARD

FINALIST

She is in the chair of honor, resplendent and nervous.
Young, three inch heels and pearls. Cocktail dress and perfectly pressed hair. The center of attention, she is not sure she wants to be that. But says: she and her lover agree, they have a fabulous life. And she does, and he does.

And we are all here for her, Bride-to-be, we future Brides and Brides of yesteryear.

Like the spirit of Christmas Past, Present and Future. We have been in that chair.

"Don't break the bows!"

"How many children will you have?"

"What are the colors for the wedding?"

"Tell us of the honeymoon plans."

I recall myself feeling nervous in that hot seat, wondering what was expected of me. It feels a lifetime ago. Or three. Was I really like her?

She gets a stock pot, the large one with a lid. "What do I cook in here?"

We tell her. We Brides of Weddings Past, who now know without a doubt what to do with a stock pot. We also know what to do with things she has not even imagined yet, sore ears of babies and lost teeth of first graders. Hormones of teenagers and achy backs of husbands.

Yes, I was absolutely like her. Eerily similar.

She is in the perfect translucent bubble of young love, soon to be newly wed, making the first home, deciding who will clean the bathroom and who gets ready first in the morning. Will we have sex in the morning or at night? Both? And who decides that, smile. And how do we make our way through life?

And how do we make our way through life?

How do we make our way through life?

There is some arc of transaction here, some reassurance that all the women around this full room have figured it out. And our stock pots are full. Chock full of Life. Stock of Life. Sometimes more than we can comfortably handle. Sometimes the soup is bitter and sometimes sweet. One of the greatest lessons is to learn to make a good meal out of what you have.

Will I travel as graciously through the next stage of life I see displayed before me here? Perhaps. Another great lesson. Be where you are because time is carrying you forward to the next wedding shower and it is not yours. Maybe it will be your daughter's, or your granddaughter's

She cries when she opens the gift from her feisty and fun Grandmother who shopped ahead for a perfect gift. You know the one, the cookbook in red plaid. It has served so many young women with good advice and recipes that are hard to ruin, easy to afford, and inoffensive to most palates. The cookbook will have to offer the advice since Grandmother is no longer able to attend wedding showers. She is in her grave now, a beloved Grandmother. I know this from her gravestone at the funeral I attended. Even more poignant, I understand this from the Bride's tear-stained face.

This is a true thing. Sometimes the soup is bitter along with the sweet. Sometimes there is less life in our pot than we want.

And there is another great lesson here, I think, of women, and time, of generations and humanity.

If you get a grasp on the wisdom I felt there in that room, can you tie it all in a bow and bring it to the next wedding shower? We are all in need of that collective wisdom and the tribe to share the journey with us.

How do we make our way through life, and how do we make our way out of it? And how do we nourish each other along the way? These are the questions I ponder as I make my own pot of soup on this cool fall day. And yes, I am making soup in the stock pot that my Grandmother gave me as a wedding present 19 years ago. And no, I am not following a recipe from my copy of the red plaid cookbook. I learned a while back to improvise and make a delicious soup from what life gives me, and from what is left over in the refrigerator. I have learned that no book can give me all the answers, but that a good pot of soup is always made better by friends and family to share it with. And that even if it is not a perfect pot, it is perfect to be together on a fall day sharing soup.

The wisest among us are grateful and thankful for all the soup, all the pots, all the wedding showers, and all the women, each as they pass. May I be one of those wise and grateful ones, thankful for both the bitter and the sweet. Thankful for it all.

Laundry

SALLY STRAP

FINALIST

"Laundry draws life's memories together in a basket."

At sixteen, after tossing my entire wardrobe on the floor, only one outfit would suffice. My treasured, but crumpled, bell bottom jeans and orange striped polyester body shirt. They needed immediate cleaning. Style at the time demanded that pants drag on the ground, covering one's feet, so the let-down hem had a ribbon cautiously sewn to cover a faded line. The body shirt, with snaps at the crotch, was critical as the low rise jeans weren't high enough to tuck anything in. My mom wasn't home that day, so the crisis forced me to learn to do laundry.

After moving to an apartment as a young woman, I remember hanging out at the Laundromat for what seemed like hours. Sitting and staring at the tumbling dryer with eyes wide open and shoulders slumped, waiting for its inevitable slow and stop.

Eventually, single life turned into a blissful married adventure. Our socks were tangled, jeans spooned in the basket. Red sleeves hugged blue plaid flannel shirts. Intimacy grew as we became accustomed to folding each other's clothes just the right way with sections under or over. We decided as a couple how to fold the soft blue towels from our wedding. It was one of life's important decisions that ranked up with gaining consensus on how to unroll the toilet paper—over or under.

I remember baby laundry, and wondering how little items the size of my hand actually fit anything human. Carefully folding each tiny sock, I lovingly placed them in the dresser that awaited our first child. I rocked in the brown nursery rocker with my hand over my belly, staring at closed drawers, dreamily wondering who was going to be born. Baby yellows and greens filled the room, as we didn't know the sex until she was born.

Oh, how the clothes and volume grew as the kids developed. From baby-spit-up to ground in mud when they helped plant a tree in the yard. Red stains from "pasgettii" night, despite a special shirt that we always put on them. Grease from who knows where, or stains from mysterious accidents. I always smiled when folding their matching OshKosh corduroy bibs with scattered, pastel handprint designs. Stain removal became a challenge in those years, taking me through many products until I grasped the power of Lestoil.

I treasured, but not enough, laundry-folding parties when the kids grew into teenagers. Folding while I listened to the chatter of their lives and we whittled the mountain range of clothes down to a mound, and then several neatly folded baskets. Off to one daughter's room to be immediately put in orderly drawers and closets. Off to another room to be set haphazardly on top of clutter. Only to be dug through in a morning crisis when decisions had to be made about what to wear. Clothes flying until the item at the bottom of the basket was found. The following week, some of those still folded clothes would be rewashed, the result of undefined piles of clothes being scooped up for the new week's laundry call.

I handled their fancy dresses gingerly after our first cruise. The girls had been so excited to get dressed up. I waded through the piles of vacation laundry, recognizing the touristy red shirt from one port and the vivid yellow sundress from another.

Rush in and out. When they were in high school, I found myself wondering if I spent more time with my daughters or their laundry. They were growing too fast as I folded laundry from their first dates, their first jobs, then their college visits. Were they really tall enough for those extra-long jeans? Did they have to buy them with holes already in them?

I welcomed laundry when the kids came home from college. Maybe it was another way to hug them each while I treasured tidbits of time with them again. We would fold while I listened to their adventures and heartbreak. Crises that seemed to be on the level of world peace. Adventures that brought ear to ear smiles in the telling.

I remember crying into soft folds of towels after the end of relationships. Divorces and "could have been" attempts at commitment. Loads of distrust with pain found in pockets as I tried to wash away strife. Inevitably, though, the last load of shared clothes came, followed by sparse white and half-full dark loads. I remember laundry being as heavy as my heart as I adjusted to a new life.

A clean basket of laundry can accompany a fresh start to life when the nest is empty. Loads of travel laundry. Loads of laundry following a visit to faraway places. Laundry following visits to daughters and their new families. Laundry preparing for the next trip, walk, or adventure. Laundry tumbling in a peaceful, quiet, and content home.

These days, the laundry basket is rarely full. The clothes are not really dirty, gently worn for grocery shopping, walking the dog, going to the gym, or sitting at my desk to write. I occasionally encounter an easy-to-remove spot or stain. Of course, there is laundry for my dog when her little striped sweaters need it.

Laundry tells a life's story that can be treasured. A story of family, love, and laughter, but also of tears shed and support given. Laundry ties together life's phases and memories. It draws life's memories of both unity and fracture together in a basket. It's always a part of life. Yes, laundry tells a story—one that is treasured.

Slowpoke

Roger Meyer
Featured Writer

A few days ago I was driving on a city street and was forced to slow down to 25 mph. I was behind one of the seven or eight drivers in the county that comply with this default speed limit.

It's not that I was in a particular hurry, it's just that I felt I had better things to do than poke along at 25 mph. And it's not that I'm really a fast driver. I seldom drive more than 10 mph over the speed limit. On the other hand, I seldom drive less than 10 mph over the speed limit.

Just before I began an internal mini-road rage scenario and began honking my horn, I spotted some tiny lettering on the license plate of the slowpoke ahead of me. It said, "World War II Veteran." After some quick arithmetic, I figured that driver had to be at least 85 years old, probably a few years older.

I looked at the driver – yep, it was an old man driving with both hands clasped on the steering wheel and staring straight ahead. I knew he was old because he didn't have a cell phone sticking out of his ear.

Then I wondered what this slowpoke did during World War II.

The Death March from Bataan killed 10,000 Allied troops. Was he one of the survivors? Or maybe he was a sailor that repaired six months worth of battle damage in three days so the *Yorktown* could fight again.

Could he have asked on D+1, why he was still alive after 2,500 other Americans died at Normandy? Or maybe he was an airman who flew through a curtain of flak and fighters to bomb the German war machine and wondered if this would be his last day on Earth.

Did he wade through a half-mile of bloody waters to get ashore at Tarawa while stepping around bodies of other Marines killed by machine gun fire wondering if this would be his last step in this life?

Could he have been one of the starving and freezing Bastards of Bastogne that fought the Panzers and Hitler's best troops with little more than a rifle and won?

Maybe he was one of the GI's that liberated a concentration camp and still has nightmares about it.

I don't know what the slowpoke did during World War II. I do know he was one of the 16 million Americans who left his family to fight for freedom.

I wonder if that old man knows how much he did for us and the people on this planet. If you get a chance to speak to him, tell him he can drive as slow as he wants to.

If I Were a Boy

MICHAELA LYNN
FINALIST

It was one of those warm spring days, the kind that only a ten-year-old kid can fully appreciate after a long cold winter, but with the bitter aroma of damp pine needles and freshly turned dirt tickling my nose, how was I to know that my life was about to change? A stiff Southern breeze kissed my pink cheeks as I stood with the other girls, watching the boys play kickball through the drone of girl chatter. They were talking about all the things normal ten-year-old girls talk about: boys, music, boys, makeup, boys, TV, and oh yeah, did I mention boys?

My attention was on Billy Mason, keeping his eye on the ball as it rolled toward him and he readied to boot it to take the lead. God, how I wished I could be down there with the boys, feeling the adrenaline, the heightened emotions of competition, the thrill of the game. But due to the roll of the genetic dice coming up double X, I was stuck there with the girls, listening to preteen female prattle and nodding my head at the appropriate times.

Becky Burton, my best friend, pointed to Billy as he rounded second. "God, he's so cute."

I watched Billy slide into third and jump up with a victory dance celebrating his daring feat of athleticism. Becky was right; Billy was certainly good looking. I couldn't deny that. He was popular, smart, and athletic. What girl wouldn't think he's cute? But as I watched the game continue–Mark Racine was now behind the plate waiting for the pitch–deep down I wished I were Billy. I could do anything I wanted. I could slide into third base to the cheers of my classmates instead of standing here, merely watching.

Becky continued to gossip with the other girls–Melissa, Angie, Lynn, Jenny (who actually wore a bra), and April–all gathered in a semi-circle with their heads together and giggling as they pointed at the boys. "Oh yeah, I bet he's such a great kisser, too."

My attention still down in the game, holding my breath as Billy crossed home, I began to wonder if the boys ever talked about the girls. Did Billy ever tell friends he thought Becky was cute? Did they discuss kissing? Probably not during the game, that was sure. From the looks of it, there wasn't time to talk aboout such nonsense as kissing and cuteness while cheering each other to a hopeful victory.

But did the boys think about those things at other times? Was Billy the ringleader, talking about how cute Becky was, with his friends nodding in agreement and giggling? I then stared across at Becky, seeing her as Billy might, so cute in her navy and white dress, blonde curls bouncing against her shoulders as she talked. How couldn't Billy think she was cute?

Becky lowered her voice and we all leaned closer. "I wish I had a boy I could kiss right now."

I don't know what came over me. Some uncontrollable force chose that moment to highjack my body. My mouth opened and I heard the words spew out as if someone else poured them out of me. "Well, I'd kiss you."

Six pairs of eyes stared back at me. Six mouths hung open. I quickly turned around, hoping to find that someone had snuck up behind me, someone else who could have blurted out such a ridiculous thing. No such luck.

April was the first to break the silence. "Wh..*What?*"

Quickly, I tried to salvage my dignity. "I just mean, you know, you're really cute. Who wouldn't want to kiss you?" I figured that should explain everything and they would now understand what I meant.

Angie took a step away from me. "Oh yuck. That's gross." She continued to gawk at me.

Now, I was beginning to panic. My face burned and I could feel a cold line of sweat trickle between my non-existent preteen breasts. I had to do something, anything, so I reached out and punched Becky on the arm. I mean, why not? Becky liked Billy. Isn't that what Billy would have done? "Hey, come on. I'm just kidding." I tried to laugh it off, a horrible grating sort of sound, hoping the six girls standing in front of me would pick up and join in.

Slowly, the other girls laughed (or maybe it was gagging, I can't be sure), but it sounded different than the secret giggles and twitters that only a second ago had floated around the group. I stared at Becky, almost pleading with my eyes for her to say something, anything, to make it all better. If only I hadn't opened my mouth. What was I thinking? What was wrong with me, anyway?

Becky stumbled back a step with her mouth still gaping open and her nose twisted up in a way I had never thought possible before then. She looked as if she were going to be sick any moment.

The awkward silence was killing me. I had to do something, right? There had to be something I could say to make this all better, so I opened my mouth only to have another rush of words pour out. "All I'm saying is if I were a boy, I'd kiss you."

Now, Becky stared at me as if I had just picked my nose and ate it in front of her. I almost had to fight the urge to do just that, anything that might get me out of there.

"God, that's sick." The whispered words came from one of the other girls– Melissa maybe this time, I couldn't be sure.

Someone else, I think it was April, muttered, "What a freak," under her breath.

Just as I opened my mouth again (I had to say *something* to fix this), the recess bell rang and the six girls turned to walk back in the school. I stood frozen, my stomach churning like a washer out-of-balance. That's exactly how I felt, too–out-of balance. Why in God's name had I said all that? Seriously, what was wrong with me? The girls, that little cadre of friends that up to then I had been a part of, shot stare after piercing, condemning stare over their shoulders as they walked away. It was at that moment that I knew I was different and would forever be different, although it would take several more years to really understand how I was different. Finally, as the boys ran past, I tore my leaden feet from the sidewalk where they felt welded to the cold April ground and with the sour taste of bile in the back of my throat, forced myself to follow.

Guide to a Happy Retirement

Patrick Cook

Finalist

I retired recently and have been feeling stressed out. I hesitate to mention it because whenever I do, my wife and friends start making sarcastic remarks about how tough lolling in a recliner must be and how much trouble it is to fill a bird feeder every other day.

One of my friends mentioned that retirement ranks among the top ten stressful situations. I was perfectly willing to believe him, but I Googled "Top Ten Stressors" just to make sure. Google obliged with 543,000 entries. That was more research than I was prepared to do, so I only looked at three of the entries. In each list, "Retirement" ranked number 10.

I was relieved to see this. At least I haven't been whining about nothing. There's my problem, right up there with "Fired at Work" and "Personal Injury or Illness."

What do all of these items have in common? They are changes. As a postal employee, I heard dozens of motivational speakers tell me change was good, that it was both inevitable and a shining opportunity. Hogwash. Every time a new machine came to my workroom floor it caused months of chaos and forced overtime. Let's not kid ourselves. Change is bad.

What is true of an automation system is true of a life-change. During my working days, I spent my time in cooperation with others, making friends and engaging in discussions of the finer points of sports and politics.

Now I work by myself. I have a list of things to do, inspired not only by my spouse, but by my own ambitions. Painting the garage is lonely work, and so is lawn care and gardening.

Desperate for human connection, I show up at my friends' houses unannounced and demand unreasonable accommodations, like brunch. Pretty soon I'll be writing crank letters to the editor of our local newspaper.

Learn from my experience. Here are some suggestions:

1) Join in some kind of group activity. A woodworking class or bird watching club can be an unforgettable experience of solidarity and fellowship. It may be useless and a waste of time, but at least you'll have company. In my writer's group, I not only find friendship, but have stepped up from piddling success as an essayist to total disaster as a novelist. Note: Avoid senior sports teams. If you will recall, they laughed you off the court when you played basketball in fifth grade. You haven't gotten any better, and jocks haven't changed a bit.

2) Interfere in your children's lives. True, they have left the parental nest and are bravely facing the world on their own. It is still never too late to remind them that they have dead-end jobs, unsuitable hairdos and poor taste in clothing.

3) Don't forget to exercise. A long walk around the neighborhood is just what you need to stay in shape. Note any violations of city ordinances. Afterward, call the appropriate department and complain.

Here are some things to avoid:

1) Adultery. This is rarely a good idea at any time of life. At your age, it's an invitation to disaster. It's expensive and, frankly, more trouble than it's worth. Besides, Viagra doesn't mix well with your coronary medicine.

2) Extensive home renovations. Come on. You're going to rip up carpet and sand floors? Make your son-in-law help you. He's young and fit, and besides, he works for beer.

3) Reflecting on past failures. Starting law school was a bad idea in the first place. That beautiful girl you lost when you were twenty-five? She's sixty now, has been married twice, and needs hip replacement surgery.

I hope this has been helpful. I have to fill my bird feeders now, and then I have a date with my recliner. It's a big, double-seated leather job, and is extremely comfortable. After my nap, I'm going to write a letter to the editor of my local newspaper. One of the streetlights is out, and the city won't do one thing about it.

A Bridge of Words

JENNIFER ALLEN
FINALIST

I was there the night he was born, my first nephew. After his mom, and dad, and nana held him, looked him over, counted his toes, I cradled him into my arms and promptly fell in love.

Nearly thirteen years have passed and that baby boy has grown. I've grown too. I've watched every stage with proud eyes as he sprouted into a toddler, a boy, a young man.

As I've watched, I've worried. Worried that someday, somehow, the bond that was formed on the night he was born will slip away. Not from my heart, but from his. Will the love I have for him hold in the teenage years, the college years, and the young man grown and married years?

How do I cradle him now, in the midst of school days, and soccer practice, and video games? In the midst of things that fill up a young man's world, yet hardly exist in mine?

The answer, I have found, like so many answers in my life, lies in the bridge and bond of words.

I stumbled upon it, really, this answer found in words, six years ago in a used bookstore. As I browsed through the stacks and shelves of books in search of a gift for my nephew's seventh birthday, I came across a book by Chris Van Allsburg titled *The Mysteries of Harris Burdick*.

I have always been a fan of Van Allsburg's writings. I love the stories and pictures that fill his books. I love that he is from Michigan, just like me. I love how he creates worlds and adventures for his readers to explore.

As I flipped through the pages of this captivating book, I found it was unlike anything I had ever read. On each page was a picture, with each picture was a title of a story, and with each title was an opening line. My imagination soared as I realized the rest of the stories were up to me.

In that moment, I knew this gem of a book was exactly what I was looking for.

I knew that my nephew would soon be growing into a young boy, then a young man. I knew that I would soon be growing into a mother with children of my own. I had to think of something to span the gap that was beginning to form between us. I knew that this book could be that something.

I bought the book and wrapped it up with pencils and a blank notebook and gave it to my nephew with the following wish for his birthday:

My Dear Boy,

I remember, like it was yesterday, the night you were born. I was there. I was one of the first ones to hold you, one of the first ones to love you, and my love for you grows stronger each and every year. May we fill the pages of this book together, and may you always know that you are loved.

When his birthday celebration came to an end, my nephew and I looked through the book together. I encouraged him to pick his favorite picture and from there our first story began. Together, and for hours, we passed the pencil and notebook back and forth. He would write one sentence, and then I would write another.

When our story was finished, I typed it up, his words on mine, and bound it neatly in a folder, one copy for him and one for me.

We gathered our family around us, and as I read our story out loud, my nephew beamed. I could see by the look on his face that it had happened. Just as I cradled that boy in my arms on the night he was born, just as I had fallen in love, my nephew now cradled our story to his chest and fell in love with words.

Six years have passed and, story by story, my nephew and I are writing our way through Van Allsburg's book. As his reading and writing skills evolve, so do our stories. While we used to write our stories one sentence at a time, we now trade paragraphs and pages back and forth, back and forth until another story is finished and added to our collection.

The co-authoring work my nephew and I share has definitely gotten harder. My nephew is increasingly busy with school, and sports, and being a pre-teen boy. I'm busy with my own little family of three, a household to run, and a writing career to tend to. We used to live just a couple hours from one another, but now three states span the distance between us. All of this adds to the challenge of our writing.

Still, the bridge between us remains, built with words, and pictures, and stories. Whether through email or the precious time we are given together, our stories continue.

Someday, my nephew's fixation with video games will fade (maybe), his school days will be behind him, and his soccer practices will come to an end. Someday, my own children will be grown, my house will be quiet, and perhaps my own books will sit on a used bookstore shelf. As my nephew grows, as I grow, many things will pass away, but a shared love of words, a shared love of each other is something that I hope will last forever.

I cannot take credit for my nephew's love for reading, or his love for words. His mom gets the credit for that. She is the one who teaches him and nurtures him with books. But I do like to think that maybe I played a supporting role. That maybe his love and talent for stringing words together was sparked on his seventh birthday.

That maybe, the love of his aunt, a classic children's book, a sharpened pencil, and a blank notebook have melded our hearts together and fanned into flame a burning passion that will never go out.

| Poetry |

Afterbirth

Hanna at Fourteen

The teen-aged daughter who last night
reminded me I know nothing about anything
—and most of all nothing about her—
this morning decided I might know something after all.
I might know where her earring landed
when it fell as she ran distance
yesterday after school.
No ordinary charm—
a gift just that morning from the first boy to give her
a token of any sort.
I imagine him, half her height,
holding out the small blue box.
I imagine her smile, her pleasure, all that light.
And so I find myself in the field behind school
searching the chill for one errant earring,
as if she might be right: a mother can intuit
where a sterling hoop hides in the grass.
It is the first morning of frost, and every blade
is stiff, silver-white and shining.
I pace the edge of the field with measured steps,
            —forward, back—
scanning for silver against the rising sun,
thinking of my daughter as she runs,
her lean strong legs, her tangled white-blond hair.

IMAGINE THIS | 89

Hanna at Sixteen

When you do something, you should
burn yourself completely, like a good bonfire,
leaving no trace…
               —Shunryu Suzuki

I draw solace from this solitude,
the labyrinth of desert grass
and dried creek beds,
a swath of Milky Way across my sleep,
the absolution of the morning stars.
Here, the world forgives—
until my distant daughter
rises from the hard red dirt,
wings white with ash, reels me
on the taut umbilical of care
and blazes:
Why didn't you Why can't you Why won't you
love me? And then my own, How could I
not?
My heart and hope, she does not see
that hers are the cells I commit
to the future, she is my lifelong lesson
in letting go.
Once, I counted moons
to when she would be born—
her body hidden in my ache
until she broke the liquid of my stretched
embrace, emerged hand-first.
Even then she could not wait
to leave.
Now her rage consumes us;
flinted words throw sparks, savage fingers flare.
She points her fierceness across skies
and years and
tinder that I have become—for her,
I burn.

Hanna at Eighteen

I rise in the dark to a full morning
moon. My daughter's eighteenth birthday,
and I am bleeding as I did
in the days after she was born. Now,
as then, my empty womb contracts.
I pause outside her room to hear
her breathing, even and steady,
think of the ways she has shared
my life-blood: all I tried to give her,
all I could not keep her from
—the way I told time
before her birth (in five moons, the baby
will be born; in two moons, the baby
will be born),
—my shuffling walks
down hospital hallways, newborn
bundled in my arms, as I murmured
I have a daughter, I have a daughter.
Her father and I vied for her
from the start, each of us wanting
the woman she would become.
She started her cycles linked to mine—
two women tuned to the same lunar score,
her young body following,
then eclipsing my own.
When, on his yearly visits, her father
tried to blunt her blossoming, she turned
her rage on me: wanting, not wanting
to be home; wanting, not wanting
to be held.
So I sit on the porch in the early
hush, sifting our splintered past. Nearby,
a nightbird cries, and I step
to the door. There, in the bare arms
of the elm, a dark bundle rests:
a Great Horned Owl—
such insistent calls, such loud silences
between. From her perch, she spreads
her wide shadow wings, catches the breaking
light and—rising—blots out
the blood-red dawn.

Kafka's Night of Mice

Wayne Lee
Finalist

–after Jacqueline Raoul-Duval

His torment begins with a sound in the sideboard,
an incessant mouse-munching on a crumb
of stale cake, a cube of muenster cheese it filched
from last night's fruit plate, perhaps an ort
of bread. Just a single intruder, but enough
to keep Franz up till dawn, to make him shout
from under his duvet and wake his sisters
down the hall, impel him to rise and scurry naked
to the door, to let the hated cat creep in.

The noises stop. Still, he cannot sleep.
Not with the smell of mouse like rancid meat souring
the room, invading his reverie. Not the idea
of mouse: mute, unclean, disgusting. The class of mice,
clandestine as proletarians. The universe of mice,
rife with suffering, pestilence, death.

A fable forms in Kafka's mind.

> Alas, the *mouse laments*. This world grows smaller
> every day. It loomed so large at first I grew afraid,
> and so I ran and ran, glad to see your chamber walls
> so far away. But now they've narrowed to a corner trap,
> and fate demands that I be caught.
>
> *Just change your path,* suggests the cat, who promptly
> captures and devours his prey.

With tale in hand, Kafka yawns and drifts serenely off.

Meditation on Water

TAHLIA HOOGERLAND
FINALIST

I am water.

I am the rain that fell on my upturned face last night.
Life-giving, thirst-quenching rain swept up into clouds
To fall again and again.
To be dew and frost,
Snow and fog,
Puddle and flood.

I am the sluggish vernal pond that holds spring peepers and teems with life.
I am rimmed with eggs and promises.
I am rich with swamp scents,
Protected by cattails.

I am the inland lake,
sparkling with sunlight,
silver rippled surface in small breeze.
Dark and cool in my depths, light and warmth in my shallows.
Minnows breathe the air I hold.

I am the moving current
of the river and stream.
My rocks are slippery with algae,
and crayfish tiptoe on my floor.
The heron's long legs pick delicately
along my borders,
and turtles sun themselves
on my fallen trees.

I am the Great Lake,
All colors and depths,
Turquoise and green,

Black and silver.
Lovely rocks tumble
With my crashing waves.
Wind whips me
While I am held
In the hands of the continent.

I am water.

I change forms.
I stay the same.
I change colors.
I hold any shape you give me.
I have deeps no one has seen,
And shallows
Visible to all.
I am cold
And warm.
I overflow,
And I shrink away,
Becoming invisible at times.
I can be wild and loud,
And soft as a ripple,
Smooth as glass.

You may disturb me
Endlessly,
But I remain
In the end
Still.

Water.

A Poem Kicked Me in the Ars Poetica and Walked Out

GERALD BARRETT
FINALIST

Last night I had an argument with a poem.
It said, "Fine," and walked out the door.
Now I worry for its safety.
I regretted what I had said.
The fear of finding it
lying in a gutter drunk
had me walking downtown
in my pajamas.

It had so much potential.
The poem thought it was finished.
I kept messing with it.
The compression plucked at its last straw.

"I don't even recognize me anymore!"

"You are overweight, heavy on the clichés
and dripping with sentiment."

"Well, I liked me. I am never good enough for you."

"Listen, as soon as I get you trimmed down
to where the reader has to squint to see you
then I will let you be."

"What about me?"

"It has little to do with you really. You are not your own."

"What?"

"You are merely a window through which to look."

"More like a peep hole the way you keep cutting me down."

"It's the nature of things to minimize the number of words
but at the same time maximize the meaning of the remaining words."

"Blah, blah, blah."

"Awe, come on now."

"No! You come on now. How would you like it if…"

"I am not a poem."

"Says who?"

"Well…"

"Ha! See, who is trimming who now?"

"Alrighty then. If you don't like the way you are treated…
there's the door."

"Fine."

Give Us This Day Our Daily Bread

JOHN GUERTIN
FEATURED WRITER

The big church brunch was 'bout to commence
In Utah's old town of Recompense,
But, they were short of bread, and in quite a fix,
'Till old Miss McGoogle come through in the nicks,
With three hundred buns that done the tricks.
Now, she knew she had doubts about her mix,
Like somethin' was odd 'bout the yeast or the flour.
But it went to the table, last tick of the hour,
A multitude served by God's mighty power.

So the congregation sat and dutifully waited,
For the Thanksgivin' blessing, and then to be sated.
But I squirmed like the devil because I was eight,
As I stared with contempt at my empty plate.
Then, above the murmurs arose Pastor Jed,
Thankin' great God for our daily bread.
He 'knowledged McGoogle, who was a bit nervous,
'Bout all those buns God had seen fit to serve us.

He said: "Thank you Lord for this splendid repast,
And blessed is McGoogle, who bakes buns fast.
Twice bless this brunch which is unsurpassed!"
"Amen!" we intoned, and could eat at last.
Now, there was stuffed turkey, 'taters 'n corn,
Ham, 'n scrambled eggs sunny as morn;
All good things reverently grown by Man,
Here in the western hinterland.
But the best thing of all is a fresh baked bun:
They was gobbled up quick by everyone.

The only complaint came from old Sy Grizz.
I heard him murmur after he bit his,
"This bun went off with the derndest fizz!"
Still, 'cause they was special blessed I reckons,
T'weren't a soul there didn't go for seconds.
But poor Miss McGoogle was sittin' on pins;
In her haste she worried she'd mixed up her tins.
She'd offered her buns, took that "thank you" epistle,
Knowin' her bromo tin was clean as a whistle.
Well, she told Bee Booker, and gossips come grumblin',
But soon t'was drowned out by a noisier rumblin'.

Now, at the end of our table sat old Auntie Daint ...
Turned so red in the face, seemed she would faint,
When a fireman come slappin' her on her back,
Like she was havin' a chokin' attack.
We all stood by helpless, a-petrifyin'
Her condition in dire need o' verifyin',
'Til she let rip a thing most terrifyin':
"Breeee-aaap!" she burped, and, "I'm fine, now," a-clarifyin'.
Then we too felt relief and a-breathin' more easy,
We jumped right back into our macaroni cheesy.

And then 'round the room, as strange as could be,
There rang out a burp bread symphony.
From brother and sister, from dyspeptic mother,
Great mighty burps, one, then another;
The loudest burps you ever heard roll,
Followed by "Pardon," and a bite of casserole.

Now, Pastor up front stood in prayerful question,
Askin' God if He'd 'scuse all this indigestion,
'Til he too was taken. He plumb give up fightin'.
He burped real loud, shrugged, and got back to bitin'.

And there 'round the head table was a sight to see,
As the church choir burped in sure harmony.
And t'was prob'ly a really fine hymn, I'd surmise,
But sure t'weren't one folks could recognize.

And when t'was near done, guests were all sheepish;
Miss McGoogle snuck out the back way a-weepish.
But I'd had the best time a boy could wish.
I stuffed another piece o' pie in my dish,
And talked about burpin' with great Uncle Reds,
And 'bout that burp music, we all shook our heads.
Now, p'raps t'was the yeast, or p'raps t'was the flour,
Or p'raps t'was bromo made that dough go sour,
But Pastor claimed the Devil got into that stuff;
Why, he'd done bless it twice, but plain t'weren't enough.

And poor Miss McGoogle couldn't stand the strain.
Folks saw her leaving on the 6:40 train,
A-readin' a cook book, quite sick with remorse.
She went to stay with Sister up in Kickin' Horse.

And the next Sunday, Pastor, in a bit of a fret,
Preached about gluttony and the sin it beget.
I didn't quite grab that, just bein' a lad,
But later that day I confessed to my Dad:
"It's a shame Miss McGoogle is feelin' so bad;
Them burp buns are the best buns I ever had!"

Why I Write

PETER DEHAAN
FINALIST

Linking letters and
wielding words to create art
for God, my patron

Once

AMY HENRICKSON
FEATURED WRITER

Once
you were there
and
I was not
until
the universe shifted
when
I caught your eye
Then
you found me
not
outside me
but
inside me
Now
you are here
and
I am here

Torched

SUSAN RANKIN
FEATURED WRITER

A completely enclosed steel cubicle stood in the middle of an empty warehouse.
The cubicle was a furnace with the door large enough for fire feeders to enter.
A raging inferno was contained inside the cubicle behind the heavy door.
She knew her father was going to enter the cubicle. He had said so himself.
She didn't know what day he would enter the cubicle. He didn't say.
Would he come out of the fire pit like Shadrach, Meshach and Abednego?
She smiled when he came home, but not when he went to work again.

She didn't feel much like playing when her father was gone.
Her mom seemed happy though; acting like Mom made her feel safer.
She hugged her father when he arrived home okay every day.
She was quiet when he went back to work the next day.
In time, she forgot to pray for her Dad and began playing again.
Her dad never came home upset again saying, "I'm going to be fired."
Angela entered kindergarten that fall right after her father had been promoted.

Night Chrysalis

GLORIA KLINGER
FINALIST

Flimsy morning light
seeps through the curtains.
I stir the bed sheets
my chrysalis warm, comforting.
I wait.
The furnace clicks on
a turbulence of warm and cold,
air masses mingling, a storm.
I wait.
Light presses in,
outlining the windows
tiptoeing across the ceiling.

Toes, fingers, eyes open
and one pale wing breaks the cocoon.
A leg bends and twists,
a steady heartbeat thrums.
I wait
on the edge of the bed
while my wings dry,
like the yawning pink-blue morning
breaking from its night-jeweled case.

Cracking Through the Cosmos

NESSA MCCASEY
FINALIST

He suddenly, surprisingly
leaned into the older, steady man
entering into a hug
that then was offered
in response to the gesture,
gratefully even.
Witness to this exchange,
I felt the tremor,
foundational,
as the man's three-ton iceberg
of frozen tears mixed
with the dross of his life and
minutely shifted.
Small purple violas sprouted.
I know I saw Paradise
in the middle of the kitchen.

| Honorable Mention |

Heat Wave 1951

LINDA LEE
HONORABLE MENTION

Somewhere on a curvy country road Mom snapped,
"Donald, pull over." Dad skidded
into field grass. Mom dumped the baby
on the seat and bolted out of the car barefoot.

We three sisters roasted silently in the back seat gaping,
while Mom yanked her blouse over her head,
dropped her skirt, sprinted along a tractor rut,
waded through reeds to launch herself into a lake.

She swam arm over arm all the way to the center
where she floated on her back.

Dad was bellowing, "Come back, Bertha Jane, damn it,
come back here now."

Mom vanished underwater. She swam to the far shore
before turning toward us.

Dad clenched his fists at his sides, helpless
among the Queen Anne's lace.
We stood in a row in the shade,
even the baby watching.

Mom drifted back, stopping to tread water on the way.
She rose from the lake with waterweed in her hair,
cow lily caught in her bra trailed across her midriff.
When she flipped her head, water sparked around her shoulders.
Peeling off wet underwear, she raised her arms to the breeze,
turned to air-dry before putting on the blouse and skirt.

She opened the car door and got in.
The children all sat in back without fighting for windows.
Donald slammed into the driver's seat, mashed the gas so hard
the wheels spun. Mom's arm flew out the window,
she turned her hand to feel it lifted like a wing.
She never did pull her arm all the way back
inside that black Chevy.

Chicago Blues Festival in Grant Park

Carol Bennett
Honorable Mention

I worked five long years for one woman and she had the NERVE to throw me out.

In the winter I remember
music, pale and faint, just sounds,
when the silent snow surrounds.

Yet in warmth of early summer
cooled by lake air through the trees,
soothing creamy eastern breeze,

in Chicago, over train yards
under steel cliffs, teasing sun,
memory and life are one.

Rhythms rich as jambalaya,
drums below horns' flying notes,
harps that squeal, guitars that float.

Music pulsing from the stages
drenches ears, then scatters, fades.
Blues around me, I am made.

Aged black men, thin legs flailing
proud in iridescent suits.
Craggy faces prove the roots

that shape their lyrics – poems of pain,
hard got love, hurt love, an itch
or a thirst no drink will quench,

songs of sadness and injustice,
rage and resignation, too
long endured to heal with blues.

Coarse voices saturate the air
blend with red beans, rice and sweet
potato pie, beer, greasy meat.

The younger men, their voices sharp,
claim their fathers' plywood thrones
with rock beats, discordant tones,

too impatient to go slow, down
deep in wailing blues to show
what it is their daddies know.

Their songs of affluence and love
requited, women who came
home again, it's not the same.

This, then, each year is my rebirth –
drums my heartbeat, horns my breath,
harp my soul, guitar my steps.

Toothless old drunk woman gyrates
her mouth open, eyes askance.
Every year, same stage same dance.

I watch her and a whirling girl
who's come undressed and, like them,
next year I'll be here again.

One of the Most Beautiful Places

E. A. WILDE CRYDERMAN
HONORABLE MENTION

In the imaginary world of Aurora Boring Alice, Alice Krupperminsk was the clerk who helped Americanize old Great-Uncle Stanley's family name, the name that had made her tougher for life. "Mm, Krupperminsky. Let's see, you could shorten that to 'Krupa,' like the boat company. Or, now, 'Copper' with the hard 'C' would be attractive. Or, how about 'Rupp,' or 'Permi.' That–'Permi'–has an important, scientific ring to it . . . So . . . what will it be then, Mr. Krupperminsky?"

"I think you can take away the ypsilon," he said. He had learned English, though British English, so he had a charming, mixed, musical accent. "Yes, Krupperminsk. Krupperminsk. I like that."

Of course, her name wasn't really Aurora Boring Alice, either. That was the nickname Michael MacDonald had called her in fourth grade at Greater Gratiot Elementary School when they were studying the atmosphere. He was also the one who once sat by her on the bus and told her somebody had bitten him that day, after which he bit her shoulder and said, "Like this."

When Alice recounted the story to Mama, she briefly thought about passing the bite along, for effect, of course. But that was what was wrong with Michael's storytelling in the first place. In the second place and third place, Alice loved her Mama Lina–short for Emilie Ottilie Marie Carolina–so much, she was ashamed to have even had the fleeting thought.

Alice was nonetheless pleased to have a bonafide nickname that did sort of refer to something beautiful. Plus, everyone knew that Alice was not boring, so it was a kind of tease that included her into most everything that went on at school. She was a quiet and good student, so no one who might later depend on her as a study buddy would be too mean.

What made her not boring were two things. She could draw anything on anything with anything and she could hum and whistle at the same time. If it was during lunch, she'd wash her thick and thin sandwich down with water and do a requested round, say, "Row, Row, Row Your Boat," or "Three Blind Mice," humming first, then adding the whistled round. Her best one was "Dona Nobis Pacem," which she'd do if someone added in a piece of licorice or some potato chips.

That doesn't include the fact that Alice also spoke two other languages besides English. To her, since she was not allowed to speak them around people who might not understand them, it was really like that part of her was invisible. Except, once in a while, she experienced "auditory delay" in responding to a question in English that was being filtered through those two other languages. People would get impatient with her sometimes or think she wasn't listening, which taught her to be very quiet, so fewer questions would be asked of her. This also taught her to be patient with herself because she was always thinking very fast and in layers. There were so many ideas and funny and ridiculous scenes that floated by as she sat listening and doodling on her papers.

She'd count how many times Mr. Williams took off and put on his reading glasses, while she thought of how many words she could make with the letters of her name.

A L I C J A S U S A N NE K R U P P E R M I N S K
AAA EE II UU C J KK L M NNN PP RR SSS
ARE SPARE PARE PAIR PAN PANS ANT ANTS AUNT AREA
SPARES PARES PAIRS PANT PANTS AUNTS AREAS SNARE
SNARES MAIN MAIL MAILS UNCLE EAR LIP LIPS CLIP CLIPS
CLAP CLAPS CAP EARS PLEASE PLEASES EASE EASES SEAM NAP
NAPS UNCLES CAN CANE CANES RULE RULES REEL REELS
SEES CANS CAPE CAPES LAKE LAKES LAME CAMERA SEE MAN
MALE MANE MANES NAME NAMES SAME SNAIL MEN CAKE
CAKES LAMP LAMPS SLIM SLIME SNAILS MASS MASSES MISS
MISSES KISS KISSES SAIL SAILS MANNER CAR LIKE LIKES PAL
PALS PAIL PAILS RAIL RAILS REEK REEKS CREEK MANNERS
CARS LAIN LAP PLAN PLANNER PLANNERS PLANK PLANKS
PLANE PAPA PACK CARE PAIN SAP SAPS MAP MAPS SMACK
SNACK SNACKS PLANES PAPAS CARES PAINS SPA SNAP PLAIN
PLAINS PEAK PEAKS SPEAK SPEAKS PRIMER NEAR PALE SNAPS
SNIP SNIPS SPIN SPINS PIN PINS PEN PENS RIM PEAS NEARS
PALES SCAM SCAMS SCRAM SCRAMS ALMS CALM CALMS
SUN RIMS PEA PEAR ALE SUNS SCAR SCARS SCARE SCARES
RACE RACES SPACE PRIM RUN PEARS ALES SEA SCAN SCALE
SCALES SPACES RANK RANKS REAM PRIME RUNS SEAR SALE
SEAS SCENE SCENES SINK SINKS INK INKS LINK LINKS
PRIMES SEARS SALES SPAN SICK SICKNESS PICK PICKS PINK
PINKS PIE PRINCE SMEAR PANE SPANS SPRAIN SPRAINS RINSE
RINSES RISE RISES PRINCES SMEARS PANES REAM REAMS
REAL LEARN LEARNS EARN EARNS

Then, if she would add the letters from "Aurora Boring," that could make more than a hundred new combinations and sentences. As Alice thought about the words she was forming from her name, each one came with at least one picture. There would be the one thing connected to the word that first–almost instantly–appeared, and then other pictures would follow. Many pictures that were connected to her other languages would dance around the words.

She would doodle on the edges of her papers including the loose leaf holes as she listened to Mr. McKnight about the perfect right triangle and the Pythagorean Theorem. Alice liked Pythagoras and Euclid and Newton. Where were the boys that turned out to have ideas with pictures and symbols like that, she wondered. It seemed there weren't very many girls with these thoughts, so Alice was quiet about that. She smiled as she designed a scalloped collar on the back of the "Estimating the Height of a Flagpole" homework assignment.

What made her laugh in school were things like Mrs. Brookley exclaiming, "My stars and steel-rimmed garters!" in English class. This kind of thing would get Alice to drawing any number of versions of stars and steel-rimmed garters, and whispery giggling. Mrs. Brookley was the one who began encouraging Alice to write about her family. She also encouraged Alicja Susanne to use her real name.

Most of all, Alicja Susanne loved music. Every day after warm-ups, Mr. Heming would introduce a song in a story, give out sheet music, and show a movie clip including that particular song. Then, they would sing it. They sang "Bali Hai," which had a mysterious quality expressive of yearning for grown-up love and exquisite beauty surrounded by swaying palm trees. They could almost feel the warm, white sand between their toes even though they were singing in a windowless cement block room that terraced down to a piano from behind which Mr. Heming's tan, bald head nodded and turned. The lenses of his black-framed glasses made his eyes look huge when they looked at the group singing the melody and then cornered left and right to keep everyone together. Once in a while, he would play the piano with one hand so he could direct with the other, but mostly it was his trusting gift to their independence that he sat down there on the bench, playing up to them with sweeping flourishes.

Many years later, when Alice was married and the mother of several children, she'd remember the thrill of "Bali Hai" and try as a grownup to reimagine the exotic beach with the warm trade winds gently caressing her cheek. For a moment, she'd wonder how that whole movie turned out, but it was almost better not seeing it because it was one of the most beautiful places she had ever been.

Green

ANDREA PONIERS
HONORABLE MENTION

On this Saturday night, Camille found herself headed for the county fair with a hoodlum called Pacer and his buddy Skin. As the Chevy pick-up crawled around the corner, Skin's leer swayed like a dim bulb behind the truck window. He pushed open the passenger door but didn't get out, so Camille climbed over his lap to get to the space between the two guys. They smelled like the cheap beer in the paper bag between her feet. No one tried to talk over the tinny radio, since Camille had nothing to say and the guys wanted to finish the six-pack—probably their second—before they hit the parking lot.

Camille had one good memory from childhood and it was the Adams County Fair. The dependable math of her family—five-divided-by-two-leaves-Camille—was in her favor there. Her mother buckled into a seat on the Ferris wheel with one sister and her dad sat with the other. Camille climbed alone into the next seat and, with the world in motion and everything a blur, she imagined a life she knew could be hers if not for pulling the short straw. She was sure it was a life others lived for more than just moments, a life that didn't require the unlikely transformation of pumpkins and frogs to have a happy ending. Camille savored the pause at the top of the Ferris wheel, her family hanging in pairs below her, her lips almost able to kiss a star.

Riding the Ferris wheel was a different matter that night with Pacer and Skin. They had left Pacer laid out behind a hot dog stand with his head propped on a bag of onions. Skin climbed into the seat next to her but was so bad off that he barely even tried to cop a feel before he began to wail and gag. He hung his head over the side but that made him even sicker, so he just let it fly down his knees and onto his shoes. He was still groaning at the bottom when the buck-toothed ride operator started cussing over the disgusting scene.

Camille slipped out of the seat and ran, knowing all too well the feeling of being asked to clean up a mess that she hadn't made but somehow would be blamed for just the same. She hurried across the fairgrounds, toward a tent with striped canvas so faded she didn't know what colors it was intended to be. Sounds escaping from an opening in the tent merged with the din outside. Camille slipped in, and out of sight of the Ferris wheel.

The long spine of the tent was hung with dusty light bulbs along a yellow cord. Arcade games sprouted like shrubs along the perimeter where teenage boys or younger tried their luck, sure that the next quarter would make them a winner no matter how many coins had already passed through their fingers.

Camille stood in place, deciding what to do next, when she was struck by the bright colors and sweet call of what could have been a rare bird migrating through this boy's camp. It was a girl, perched next to a boy, who was propped against a Skeeball machine.

The girl was tall and leaning forward at the angle of a hand about to pat a puppy. She laughed again, that trilling bird sound, and Camille thought she saw it ripple through the sunset colors of her halter top.

The girl lifted an arm, slender as a foal's leg, and placed a single fingertip at the collar of the boy's black t-shirt. His eyes narrowed and they both laughed, bird and beast. As the pair moved to face the Skeeball game, Camille ducked behind a darkened fortune teller's booth, its electrical cord hanging over the top like a tongue gone mute.

She watched as the boy shoved coins into the machine, releasing three balls into the trough at their knees. He swirled a ball around his open palm like he had the whole world in his grip, then reached for the girl's hand. As she moved forward, her hair fell back over her bare shoulders. It was the color of pecan pie and glistened as if it might be covered in a sugar glaze. Keeping her eyes on the girl, Camille tucked her own hair behind her ears, catching a tangle and tugging it free.

The boy placed the ball in the girl's hand, wrapped his fingers over hers, and stepped behind her so their frames fit like nested boxes. Camille touched her shoulder where the black shirt would meet her checkered blouse. She moved her other arm back slowly as their arm—the boy's arm and the girl's arm, swinging with the single motion of an oil rig—moved toward the Skeeball ramp. Their hands opened, the ball released, and the girl lounged back into the boy to watch and wait. They held their breath, the three of them, as the ball rolled up the short alley and circled into the hole marked "0." Camille bowed her head, begging forgiveness from the boy, who obligingly kissed the oven-warm brown bangs before sliding a hand across the seat of the girl's jeans, rounded like the breasts of doves.

He reached for another ball and Camille shook her head as the girl feigned protest. The boy turned her toward the machine again, stealing a taste of her neck. Camille muffled a sound and steadied herself against the fortune teller's booth. They released the second ball, which skidded forward and again disappeared into the hole marked "0." Camille buried her face in her hands. When she looked again, the girl was shoving the boy toward the machine, her fingers spread wide against his broad shoulders. He casually tossed the last ball up the ramp, where it bounced once before dropping cleanly into a hole. "25." Camille hugged herself as the girl's hands found the inside of the boy's back pockets to pull him toward her.

The game was over. The boy and girl turned to leave, their shoes disturbing dust around the trampled weeds inside the tent. Camille stepped silently where the couple had just walked, out of the tent and between brightly lit food stands. She came to a stop next to a hanging net full of lemons, big and solid as a punching bag, the bulging fruit seemingly brighter than fruit could ever be.

The girl was pointing to a sign for twenty-one flavors of icy slushes. Camille was lost in the decision when they were interrupted by a trio of guys, bigger and sloppier than the Skeeball champ. Their voices were deep and dumb, disturbing the air as they approached.

"Where you been?"

"We been lookin' for you!"

The girl brought her hand to the boy's shoulder, but he took a step toward his buddies and her arm swung down through space before she could stop it and reach back up to catch a rope of her own thick hair. Camille wrung her hands behind the bag of lemons and waited.

"It's about time," the boy said, his voice changed from the soft Skeeball tones. "I already gave up on you." His eyes darted toward the girl but returned to his friends. "Where we goin'?"

Two of the goons started talking at once, their arms moving as if it meant something. The third guy rubbed his belly and studied the list of sweet slush flavors. The girl took this moment to tuck a finger under the boy's belt and move her mouth toward his ear. He jerked as if he had been bit, splashing a hot look across the girl's face, and Camille turned from the sting of it. "Let's go," he said to the guys. "I been waitin' for you all night." Their voices, a commotion, stayed behind as they moved toward the midway.

Camille and the girl waited until thoughts could rearrange into the next moment, when action was required. The ends of the girl's hair caught on a passing nylon jacket, creating cobwebs that paused and broke in mid-air. When the girl turned, Camille saw her blue and glistening eyes, her chin that twitched as she bit her lower lip. She turned again and slipped silently into the passing crowd.

Camille kept her in view, stretching into the aisle until she lost her balance, then righting herself with such force that she fell against the bulging bag of lemons. It swung back freely at the touch and bumped her lightly on its return, exposing the deceit of perfect plastic fruit.

It was midnight. She wandered until she found Pacer still among the onions, with the car keys dangling from his long index finger. Camille snagged them and scanned the faces in the dwindling crowd for Skin's bony jaw, as Pacer struggled to right himself among the burlap sacks.

Stargazer

AMANDA WILSON
HONORABLE MENTION

And then I reach above my head into the starry night,
Stretching, stretching high to grasp the shining specks of light.
Look there! One sparkles near my palm, close enough to touch,
Dancing in the empty air like diamonds, glass, and such.
I close my hand around the sphere; it burns and chills like ice,
Prickling, tingling, draining warmth, my fingers pay the price.
I reach again into the sky to catch another star.
I lift my feet above the ground, they dangle where they are:
Hovering in time and space, the Earth a foot below.
I look above me to the moon, its pallid face aglow.

Then I begin the steep ascent, climbing to the sky.
My footholds feel like smooth, round stones. I kiss the stars goodbye.
Hand over hand, foot over foot, humming as I go,
Faster as I near my goal, the moon appears to grow
Closer still until I stop and place my hand upon the stone.
I lift myself onto the surface, content in the unknown.

I sit upon the frozen orb, watching planets turn,
Marveling at the distant sun and how ferociously it burns.
Look up and to the west! There are my friends, the twins:
Castor and Polydeuces, where the Milky Way begins.
I rode with them on silver horses up to Mount Olympus,
Then six months later, crossed the River Styx with souls beside us.
I ran from deadly Scorpius with Orion at my heels.
I know how cold the icy surface of Europa feels.